An Unsung Ballad

A Vitki's Memory

Written & Edited By:

Bryce Carlson

Dedicated to My Loving Grandmother, Karen. The one who started my writing adventure.

"Wealth dies. Friends die. One day you too will die. But, the thing that never dies is the judgement on how you have spent your life."

-Hávamál

PROLOGUE

She sat there, hair unfurled into a mess, the usual way she always had it, not properly groomed, still wreaking of the mountains of ice, she held no contempt to please the Aesir any more than she had to; she was a Goddess now, no longer just a giant of the icy regions of Jotunheim. Her Father was their king in that world, until the Aesir took his life. She was now akin to the fellow Gods in Asgard, though out of familiarity, she was still under dressed. Skadi was to marry into the Aesir — out of an apology for killing her family.

She sat silently on the wooden benches hand carved by the Sons of Ivaldi — talented dwarves that hid in the lower mountains of Asgard. They were recognized by their grace and craftiness of their works and dedicated it all for the Aesir and Vanir; from constructing the many halls of Asgard, the rafters down to the shiny floor made of gold, to the crafting of small runes that shimmered to every passing torch, and when struck, the whole halls lit up.

"Another drink of mead is fine by me!" Sang the drunken dwarves together on the opposite side of the long table. She smiled as they clashed their cups together drunkenly.

Their greasy and oily hands pitch black from the rest of their body. A night of clashing steel with hammers, and sweating from fires, they were letting loose. "Been a Boar's age, Sindri!" Brokk said pouring some more into his mug, "Damn fine mead it is to be shared," he was slurring a little more each splash of mead that went into his cup.

"Still wired shut, eh?" Said Sindri dampened by his Brother's mead, "Serves him right," he coldly said eyeing down the God known as Loki who could not say anything, but still had the liberty to move around as he willed. The God just peered back at him colder even colder.

His eyes deadly and mischievous for his own good — he was plotting something, the dwarves were too drunk for their own good to see it, the Gods were too busy welcoming in their new kin, but Hod could see right through it, even though blind, he knew something was stirring the Trickster.

"You cannot speak to me, I cannot see you, but I sense trouble within you," Said Hod looking blankly out into the large hall. His eyes glassy from the blindness that he was born with.

Loki just looked back at the tall Aesir with wicked eyes. If he could have spat at him, he would have, but the golden wires kept his mouth from speaking. They wired them shut, the Ivaldi Brothers did after he ripped out Sif's hair. A form of punishment Odin specifically thought would do at that time.

Hod did not say anymore. He stood tall and too appeased from the celebration. He held no love for Loki, but only sympathy for his own torment. He could feel the anger, the angst that built up in him. To have him around the others who sentenced him to his torment was just more humiliating for him. His eyes specifically staying on Baldr, Hod's brother, and Odin's son.

Loki, out of hate for Odin at the time, only thought of revenge and how he could get to the Old Man himself. Hod was too sad for him. Hurting a cripple would even be too pitiful for Loki. Too easy at that.

That is why he kept his sights on Baldr; an invulnerable God, but an easy target. Mistletoes! Anything mistletoe would puncture his impenetrable body like a sword through a paper. It would do for Loki.

"You're new to this tribe, our families," Odin started while sitting tall, one eye on the prisoner, Loki, "You are wondering about the tall one over there next to my son, are you not?" Asked Odin picking up his horn of mead to his lips that hid under his gray beard.

"Why are his lips wired?" Instantly asked Skadi still looking at Loki, his eyes back to Odin, "and why is he staring so hatefully towards you?" She did not feel scared from it, only concerned for Loki himself. Giants would have never done this to a fellow Giant. Their punishments were more swift, a quick beheading to call it a day. This was new to her.

"He ripped the roots out of another's hair. We fixed his doings, as usual. It led to that, the final twig in a brush of kindling," Odin rubbed his beard, stroking it intently while thinking of what the fiend in the corner was thinking.

"And you wired his mouth shut?"

"We did. His excuses would not stop. It was his final warning," Odin set his mead down, staring more firmly at Loki. "He has done too much to us. He will have to live with this now," Odin let out a sigh, not out of relief, but out of not knowing what the future would bring now. The dishonorable acts of Loki pushed him farther this time, where no compassion left to loosen his ropes of sympathy.

Her concern for him grew to absolute passiveness. She did not feel for him anymore. She remembered why she was there and how much change she needed to adapt and emotions were always a barrier.

She picked herself up from the bench to go mingle with her newly appointed husband, Njord, the man with the biggest feet out of all the bachelor's that were chosen for her.

"What do you feel for that man over there?" She said facing her husband, nodding her head to Loki who impatiently picked at the wires that dug into his mouth.

"I'm a Vanir. We already have our opinions of him," Njord said while bringing his horn up to his mouth, pausing from what he had to say next, "and we do not trust him."

"Why do the Aesir keep him around?"

"He's good for them. He can handle a blade, his knife. He's made to deceive. That makes him a good ally," he finally drank the rest of his mead and wiped the froth that stuck to his mustache. "Just don't get mixed up with him. He does not mean well."

Njord walked back to a table where ale, mead, and boar legs sat for the Gods. It held a natural fragrance, and beautiful organic colors that shined off of the round silver wood. The wood was from the deep forests of Jotunheim itself to help remind Skadi that her home will always be close.

She watched her husband pick the meat from the table to his platter. He ate a lot, but never filled, never grew—none of the Gods did. They had all held an inequitable physique. She found that interesting.

"Why do you not eat?" Asked Hod sensing his brother's presence, and not a drop of boar staunch on his breath, he sniffled, smelling for more, "Why do you not drink? It is a celebration." He kept his stance as if Dwarves carved him his own statue and it talked.

"You notice too much, brother," said Baldr back on the opposite side of Loki. He silently sought out Hod's wisdom he had. His Father, Odin was too distracted by the festivities around him. "I cannot help to think these dreams are true."

The dreams were of his death, of him in Hel. They were full of tangible feelings; death, pain, and agony that wrought his whole body. They happened every night he fell to sleep. Every time he closed his eyes. All too real for him.

"You cannot die though," Hod said back now looking into his eyes blankly. It always made Baldr feel a little more as if his blind brother could actually see, as if it were all a jest.

"You know I can't. They know I can't. I feel though as if I can," his face dropped to his chest, he tried to hold back his concerned eyes from turning red of tears, "everyone has their weakness."   "

"True, but no one here besides Odin, Mother, and you," he looked at Loki who pretended not to listen, he frowned to the sight of it. He knew he knew and that is what upset him.

Baldr just patted Hod on the back and started walking away from his blind brother and Loki who was now smiling, knowing what had to be done. Loki loved exploiting everyone, he loved showing that the Aesir can be weak.

Skadi slowly walked to see Loki for herself, she wanted to meet the man herself. She smiled at Hod not realizing he was blind until he laid his own foggy eyes into hers, "Skadi," he greeted her with no emotion, "Enjoying your new husband?"

He knew she wanted Baldr, his brother, the most handsome of the Aesir. Everyone usually did. He sensed her disappointment when the blankets came off of Njord's face. She was still happy about it, but greed was a Giant's number one weakness.

"He is good," she said back bringing a horn of mead to Hod, "I brought you some drink," she handed it out hoping he would find the horn. She felt weird handing a blind man something.

"Thank you. I am parched," he thanked her with a nod that showed he was not some man made of stone. "Do not mind him though, he cannot talk." He was referring to the wired Loki who mockingly curtsied to her.
She just looked at Loki and smiled, artificial but somewhat meaningful.

She saw his eyes, they were fueled by anger and resentment, and she saw it and it made her more defensive. He looked her down like an animal about to strike. She kept wondering why they kept him around and not locked up.

Loki mumbled something, blood from one of the wires that hung loose from his lower lip came trickling down. A Horrific scene, but Skadi had seen worse. It was just barbaric to her, the slow torture, and the humiliation he was enduring.

Deep down, it did not bother Loki, for he always had a way to get out of his own mess.

She turned around to walk back to the table, to sit down next to Odin and the rest. Hod felt Loki's heartbeat, it was getting louder and louder, faster and quicker. He was up to something and only the Blind man knew.

"Why are you filled with excitement?" Hod immediately turned to Loki, who was now gone. His heartbeat still where he stood. Hod looked around hoping he could sense him, but when he felt out to the spot Loki vanished from, he felt him once more with the now slower heartbeats.

Loki mumbled back to Hod, "I-mmm, here-mmm, time-mmm," he smiled at the blind God with more blood dripping from his wired mouth. He was waving a branch of a mistletoe in front of him, mocking him for not being able to see what was going to happen next. He dropped a cup of mead onto himself.

Loki quickly went to creating something sharp out of the mistletoe. He carved it into an arrow, the head of it, like a dart with his finger nails. He smiled the whole time happily. He was about get Odin back for this one. I always win.

"You seem nervous, Loki. What are you doing?" Hod could not keep his eyes off of him, he smelled the room for any signs, but he only brought in the mead that Loki poured on himself. "You spill?" Said Hod still sniffing, he let out a laugh, "Your mouth is wired shut!" He laughed again thinking Loki became clumsy and eagerly tried to drink mead.

Loki made a shrug to him as if he was just a fool for trying. He played well along with Hod's senses. He again, was a smart ally, but now someone pushed too far that made him no longer one.

He looked at Hod's brother Baldr with hate not for him but his Father. He wanted Odin to suffer for this, he wanted him to know not to ever punish him again. So he pulled his hand back, right in front of Hod and shot the dart right to Baldr.

After that, the room fell silent. A circle was formed around where Baldr had stood, but now laid dead, blood streaming from his neck. Odin cried out, first with anger, then sadness. Tears streamed his eyes like the blood that fell from his Son's neck.
Thor and

Tyr rushed to the silent, blind brother, Hod who did not know what had happened until they spoke. He pleaded his case, but more so kept quiet, for he knew the only wisdom they would gain out of this death, would be their own sins.

Loki was gone. He never returned that night. They punished and put Hod to death for the death of Baldr, for it was what would start the end of the worlds.

The night was supposed to be in celebration of a beautiful marriage, and the peace of the Aesir and the Giants, and even though the peace was carried through, the betrayal of a brother and kin was now what was focused on. As time went on that night, Odin could not think of his son's pleas, yet still remaining complacent, he knew he had done something wrong.

He did not seek his inner intellect, he only held on to the rage of seeing his other son be killed by a mysterious mistletoe dart that shot out from where Hod stood.

The more he looked in himself for answers, for wisdom, for the knowledge he needed to redeem himself from the murders, he needed to kill Loki.

<u>**1**</u>

Ahlifer sat inclusively at the end of the long
fishing dock, it stretched far into the sunset and mountains
that bordered the ocean, along with his imagination. He was
kicking his feet in the water, staring out into the sun that fell
to the edge of the water.

Stars were starting to peak out, gradually
plopping out into the growing dark sky. Night was coming,
and so was the moon and that would keep the small fishing
village illuminated for the night's fishing. He and his sister

were too young to fish by boat, but they did what they could by the dock.

The rain softly, calmly started to drop, hitting the crystal blue water and tapping the head of the little boy's amber hair. He looked up with his bright blue eyes matching the coming night's colors. He stared above, infatuated with the refreshing droplets, the day was hot and he needed this.

He wondered where the rain came from, why it came, and why now. The men would begin fishing soon and it was perfect timing for the change of weather, fish tend to bite more at night, more with rain as well.

He thought of Thor beating his Hammer on golden drums creating the rain, an oncoming storm. He thought of Ullr casting his pole into the middle of the Asgard Sea, he imagined all of it so vividly.

His imagination was abruptly interrupted by the mild sounds and shakes of the dock swaying, he looked back at what it could be. Inga, his sister was stomping her way towards him, bucket in hand held by a rough twine made rope.

He laid on his back looking more curiously into the stars, each perfectly designed to be, his imagination took off again—adventure he could not fathom.

"What are you doing?" Asking Ahlifer sensing his sister closer to him, eyes closed towards the sky.

"Fishing, what does it look like I'm doing? It's raining. Fish are hungry. So are we," said Inga while bringing the bucket close to her chest and the fishing pole to her shoulder. She was much more of a serious counterpart to her brother Ahlifer.

Ahlifer kept quiet knowing his sister would say something sarcastic to him, or simply criticize his overly-intrusive imagination. He scooted himself up from his back, shifting himself over for a spot for his sister. She set the bucket in Ahlifer's lap, water splashing onto Ahlifer, he did not complain because it wouldn't do any good.

She hooked a big worm, still covered in dirt to a piece of iron that curved into a hook... Ahlifer carefully set the bucket on the water watching it bob up and down, mesmerizingly captured by the motions he started to picture a small boat, the bucket floating on the edges of Jotunheim. One eye peering into the distance turning the surroundings into the shores of the Giant lands.

"Ahlifer! Just fill the damned bucket, please," said Inga annoyed.

He snapped out of his dreaming trance, gave a quick nod and proceeded to dip the bucket into the water; watching it slowly fill up with water, drowning underneath the atmosphere.

The bucket slowly traversed to the bottom of the ocean, still motion. He grabbed the rope just in time, lifted it with all his strength back up, and dutifully setting it in between him and his sister. He sighed with relief to escaping another conflicted Inga.

She guided the hook down into the water, about five feet away from her. The line was loose, wasn't weighted and couldn't cast more than a couple feet away from her. The wind helped, it glided the string a little farther out where fish would tend to bite more. She saw the fresh bait disappearing down low while Ahlifer watched the worm spiral, wriggle and sink.

She joined him, sitting down on the end of the dock right next to him stretching her long legs out, setting them silently into the ocean.

She was taller than her older brother, and much more mature, well, mature being more in touch with reality, where her brother was much older but he was always stuck in his imaginative mind.

The string of horse hair was attached to a long, flexing oaken branch, hand-carved perfectly for a pole. A piece of dried wood sat above of the water acting for a bobber, it bobbed up and down carefully, under, above, under, above.

The kids both stared at the end of their pole, wide-eyed with anticipation of their upcoming dinner. The rain started to drop harder onto the glass like water, the droplets smearing the surface like an oil painting.

The small gusting winds danced with Inga's fishing line, making it look as if millions of fish were present beneath. Inga was careful not to tug the line out.

No, she knew better than to act so excessively, instead she watched it, eyeing it, waiting. Her brother on the other hand was much more impatient.

"Inga! I think they got the worm," Ahlifer excitedly said setting himself up onto his knees. "Inga! I think you got a bite!" During these fishing moments, he was always on edge, excited, overly enthused about everything. Curiosities of what breed of fish she would pull up to the wonderment of what if she pulled something else up and it was not a fish.

His imagination was always on a run, his mind always bent towards the surreal, it made Inga mad when the task was always so simple.

"No," she said rescinding her brother's comment. "Quiet," she was stoic, her prose matched her stature. She waited for the fish like the hunter she was taught to be.

His eyes still peering on the end of the branch, he watched his sister move the pole into a plucking motion, bobbing the dried driftwood below the line creating a dancing motion. The worm danced underneath, teasing the fish that wouldn't bite on the worm, guiding as a puppet.

The rain now heavily dropping creating much more stronger splashes, waves began to turn, the dock began to unevenly creak.

She took a deep breath turning her impending angst into calmness. She knew they would start to feed now, the rain has spoken.

Ahlifer still intensely watching the water, the deep blue, trying to find the worm that was now invisible underneath. He clenched his fists pushing himself higher onto his knees more, giving him more depth in his sight, he wanted the fish to hook.

"Inga! Pull!" He yelled swearing to himself he had saw the drift wood bobber submerge more than three seconds. He was right, it did, it stayed under—and with that Inga rose on her feet, bracing herself for her catch.

"Get the bucket ready!" She said playing with the fish letting some slack off onto the line. She played the fish just like how her father fought in battle; giving the enemy, the fish lenience, letting it believe it won, until you finally were able to diminish its strengths, eventually feeding on the lesser energy of the target and reeling it in.

Ahlifer stood himself up soaked by the rain, he brushed his hair out of his eyes and looked into the water, bucket cupped to his chest. Inga fought and fought with the fish using her precise wits do the work.

The kids, drenched with the rain took no consideration in the uncomfortable dampness, they were too focused on the fish. Ahlifer saw the fish jump, closer now, he eased himself back down to his knees, holding the bucket close hoping it would jump to him.

Ahlifer lied down onto his stomach to be able to survey the under waters easier, and the fat, shiny fish that was caught on his sister's line. He put his hands into the cold water, trembled a little from the ice cold water. Inga backed up, positioning herself farther away for it to be easier for her brother to grab.

He saw it come closer, reaching farther in, head above the water, smelling the fish, and the salt of the sea. He brought in air and sunk his head under the water. His eyes stung from the salt immediately as he opened them. He saw the fish snagged, fighting its last fight, he reached out closer to it and dove in.

"Ahlifer!" Inga cried out trying to hold back her insensitive laugh. She felt the fish tighten on her line. She saw the silhouettes of her brother hugging it. "My Gods." She never saw her brother this desperate, full of bravery, stupidity, but still bravery. She laughed.

Ahlifer sunk with the fish that was half his size, grasping it around its ribs. He fought to subdue it, but it wiggled and shook trying to get out of its impending submission.

He was heavier than the fish, so it brought them both down to the ocean floor. He let his body weight do the work, he held tightly onto it still sinking.

His adrenaline deterred his oxygen levels giving him a little more of the upper hand. His hopes not to drown turned his innocence into survival.

He grabbed a rock on the bottom of the ocean floor and slammed it on the fishes head trying to knock it out, but his strengths were nothing down underneath. He finally squished his hands over the fish's strong skull and cracked it, instantly killing it, watching it still hooked be pulled to the dock. He swam back to the surface.

He plopped his head up out of the water, treading in place laughing to the now down pouring rain. He felt invincible, never expecting himself to pull it off from the start.

His overflowing confidence now shining through his bright smile at his sister. She did not smile back, she kept her same stoic, expressionless face on the fish that was now on the dock.

"Nice catch, Inga," he said trying to get some recognition from his sister.

She just looked over at her brother swimming in the cold water shaking her head.

"Get out of the water. You're going to get too sick to eat our catch," she said.

"Help me up then," Ahlifer said while reaching a hand out towards her. His sister would always play games with him. He did not like it, but it grew on him. She knew how stubborn she was and how headstrong.

"No. Swim to the shore."

Ahlifer shook his head, rebelling his sister's words, but she would not give in, so he began paddling around the dock towards the shore with her walking beside him on the dock laughing proudly as he stayed drenched.

Seeing her brother in such a predicament made her cheery; she loved her brother, but like all sibling relationships, especially like Inga and Ahlifer's, it always brought a sense of unnatural warmth to either one's heart when seeing the other in such a mess.

"The docks long," said Ahlifer panting still ferociously treading still. The rain blinded his sight and made the ocean far harder to swim in. He could barely catch his breath; rain water dousing his mouth, and the lack of strength in his arms.

"You'll make it," she smiled.

Ahlifer started to swim, frustrated even more, counting each board that made up the dock. *1 board, 2 board, 3 board,* his arms started to ache even more.

"I feel my arms giving out. Just pull me up, Inga," he stopped his count mid-swim glaring his feisty green eyes at her.

"You want to be a warrior someday. This is how you grow muscles, Ahlifer. Maybe after your swim, you'll have big enough muscles to go raiding with the older men," she laughed still walking ahead, rain dropping harder.

Ahlifer stopped again, sticking his toes outward towards the bottom of the ocean looking for some sort of place to catch a break.

Nothing but more water. He wished he were a fish, oh how that would have helped right now. Inga walked back towards him feeling pity for her older brother. She set her rod and bucket on the dock.

"I will help you this once, but help will not always come," she said scooting herself lower onto her knees, reaching out a hand towards him.

Ahlifer started to swim slowly towards her, he felt a slight relief, but still some embarrassment for his scenario, and he caught a fish! Barehands and all! If his Father would have seen it, he would have been handed *Runsaar,* his Father's Axe right at the exact moment.

His bravery diminished, so did his courage thinking about it. It's not the first time he has been put in such a situation fishing with his sister.

He went for his sister's hand until he felt something touching his leg, whisking by as if it were a snake hunting Ahlifer's little chicken legs. He panicked to that, he hated the sight of anything without limbs, and he quickly grabbed her hand and started to hoist himself up.

Inga wasn't strong enough so she lied on her stomach for more brace, she grabbed his arm with her other hand, until she saw what had swam by below; a dark, shadowy hand covered in moss began to clamp on her brother's leg.

"Ahlifer! Something is below!" She cried out using all her strength to pull him up, but she felt the hand pull him from the other end. "It's too strong."

"What in Thor's name!" Ahlifer gasped while looking below him seeing the dark hand slowly disappear with his left foot. "What in the Gods' names!"

He was instantly pulled below kicking and clawing towards the surface, but sank nonetheless. His muscles were now depleted of energy. He screamed under water, bringing bubbles to Inga, submerging deeper into the dark bottoms.

He opened his eyes seeing the hand crawl up his tunic, although he didn't feel it, he saw it. His eyes blood shot red from the salt, fear began to drown him, his mind convoluted with wretched anxiety.

He closed his eyes again, flashes of light to blackness back to light, so on and so forth. He began to fill the water fill his lungs, he was going to die. He felt the hand with his own trying to yank it free, following it with his fingers down to a face— of his own.

He stared at his ghastly doppelgänger feeling the racing emotions inside him, he did not know what he was looking at, but he knew it was himself. The duplicate stretched its mouth with its hands, pulling the skin off of its body, revealing a mangled distortion of Ahlifer, grotesquely revealing the inner skeleton.

He was paralyzed from what he had seen, also stunted by something else, a force he himself could not comprehend. He twisted and turned in horror trying to break free away from the image of himself deteriorating, being fed to the bottom feeders of the lake; fishes, minnows, and even snakes, he watched them all circle around the flesh.

He kept breathing, gasping under water, feeling the water pour in. By now, his lungs should have collapsed leaving his own self to die like the sailors who lived for the sea. Death, if a feeling, he felt it, there was nothing else to correlate with such.

He heard his sister scream for him up above, the dock's rickety boarding aching as she stomped around in search of her brother.

He closed his eyes hoping for an end, he prayed to the Gods' hoping for a quick death, but nothing was answered besides a voice inside his head with a response of a deep giggle.

"Why do I not die?" He replied hearing the churning of water, deep sea ocean winds push the waves underneath. His heart hurt, his lungs burned, his mind stayed numb while he soothingly asked again, "Why do I not die?"

Another hideous laugh, "Because you are not ready to die," now said a voice, his own voice.

"But I feel it."

"Feel death? Boy, you cannot feel something that does not exist," the voice sneered echoing the deep monotonous voice that hid behind, humiliating Ahlifer's own piteous existence.

Ahlifer floated as if he was slowly transpiring into Hel itself, his arms hung high, but felt anchored and his legs dangling down, but feeling as if they were tightened by a rope.

He felt the oxygen leave his brain, the water swarm his organs. Hallucinations, images of past experiences started to play through his mind, imagery so sharp as if he was there. He shook his head, or so he thought he did to rid them away.

He imagined Inga gathering the older men, them coming for his safety, words, unkind and sympathetic being thrown around among them.

He imagined Edvar, his father's old friend, and Tillu bringing swords and axes by the narrow. He did not know what else to imagine, but besides them finding him drowned all for one fish.

"Do not close your eyes now," said the voice repeatedly, "Do not close them."

"I need to die."

"You are not ready to die," said the voice ending with a small laugh. "For most of your Gods' will not allow it."

"What are you?" Said Ahlifer back to himself eyeing down the shadowy hand that grew from the bottom of the ocean.

"It is none of your concern, more so the others," said the voice back now much more serious. "I must go now. You will live, but remember this exact feeling, death you call it, remember I am your key to new life and as you are to me. You are just a pawn, a pawn that will move the right squares as long as you listen to your king, I as your King."

He saw his dissected mirage disappear, releasing his legs from the shadowy moss covered hands.

The water slowly drained out of his lungs, his heart started to pump a normal speed. He peered up to the surface, still rain tapping on it, and floated, wearily towards safety.

He shut his eyes once more determined he wasn't going mad, that he did not dream it all. He felt a tug on the collar of his tunic, being lifted out of the world below. He closed his eyes once more, feeling sleep consume him.

$\underline{2}$

The room was illuminated partially by two torches which sat on both sides of the door, hung by a metal holder, Fjorn made them back in his smithy days. There were lanterns set upon the side of the bed where Ahlifer lied resting, still in slumber.

He trembled to each rain drop that seeped in from the top of the wooden roof. Rain was once peaceful for him, now it haunts him, reminding him of the figure below the ocean.

Fjorn was on the other side of the door, sitting on an intricately designed table they supped as a family each night. He looked at the dimly glows bouncing off of the iron cups and dishes in front of him, lost in thought. His boy drowned, but remained alive. An act of the Gods or pure luck? He couldn't decide, for his decisions were distant for him due to the perturb feelings that grew.

Inga sat quietly, saying no word to her Father. She saw the sadness, the concern feeding at him. His eyes glistening with tears from the nearby light that swayed through the room.

She remembered him almost losing him two years ago, him playing by a fire on a hunting trip, a forest boar piercing his tusk into his stomach, blood wreaking from his abdomen — that is all she remembered from then.

The memories of death were a torment for old Fjorn; his wife, who died in bed from no causes, just simply relieving herself from the mortal life — for the villagers would say, while some would say curses besieged her that night.

"He saw a ghost," Inga said trying to break the nerving silence. "Of his own self," she sounded mad when the words leaked out her mouth.

Her Father stayed quiet, still, grabbing a jar of mead and pouring it into one of the iron cups. He wasn't much of a drinker, but when situations like these arose, especially his wife's death, he couldn't resist, it is how he coped through it. The first drink would mean a month's of binging, Inga knew that.

"His act of courage brought him into the lake," she said again trying to get her Father to say something, anything that would ease her mind, and maybe his.

They sat quiet for an hour more patiently waiting on news of Ahlifer. The village shaman, dressed in wolves garbs who only worshipped The Sun and Moon, *Sol and Mani* took care of him. She dressed him in herbs, moss, and other particulars to ease his pain. She would be the first to know if these events were truly a curse.

Fjorn was drunk by the mead, Inga still quiet watching her Father drink as if it were in celebration, but the tears and sorrow were a great indication that this was no celebration. She looked around the room, seeing the winds pound against the cabin, hearing the creaking of the old wood turn to every brush. She saw the farthest lantern give out its light.

The winds roared even louder, rain splattering, and hammering on the roof. Storms were common on their island, always damaging to an extent, but the people knew how to maintain it after such weather.

"A ghost," finally said Fjorn, head in one hand while the other occupied his drink of mead, "No such thing exists on this island. Over the bridge maybe, but here, no signs."   "He saw himself, that is the last thing he said, a ghostly mirage of himself," said Inga trembling from the cold that grew inside their little house. She huddled herself next to the only lit torch that hung on the wall, her father too drunk to relight it.

"Inga, ghosts do not live under the waters," he said reimagining the times when boats had sunk, delivering the souls of the dead to the sea. He only said they did not for his own personal terrors. "Ghosts do dwell across the bridge, but not in our village, only seagulls, boars, and other likely creatures, but ghosts? Do not be foolish. Your mind runs just like your Mothers."

Inga never met her Mother, but she has heard stories, one of the first women to take part in a fight across the seas. She had the same nose as her as well, which brought memories of warmth and sometimes closure for Fjorn's perturbed mind.

Inga saw the mead do harm for his racing thoughts, especially the remembrance of her father's dead wife, her mother.

"My mind is fine, Ahlifer only said that, that is what he saw. I do not believe in ghosts, they are the past's wants of life," she said stubbornly to her father in spite of his allegations. "Just like you wanting Mother back! About to lose Ahlifer, the thought of losing him, you drink to lose those ghosts, or future ghosts, but you can't focus now," she said sliding up from her chair removing herself from the room.

Ahlifer shook in his bed to the sounds of the voice laughing, humiliating him, and twisting his fears into rage. His body churning terrifyingly, seduced by the touches of death. The shaman took notice quite quick, raising her hand in the air humming a soothing sympathy of words no mortal man could understand. Fjorn ran in drunkenly, stumbling to the sight of his boy's grief.

"Stand by me, Fjorn," said the shaman quietly still focusing on her incantations.

"It is time to wake up, boy," said the voice thunderously in Ahlifer's mind. Ahlifer heard it, threw himself up, throwing up water and bile onto the floor next to him. Fjorn and the Shaman threw themselves back at the notion, seeing Ahlifer sitting up straight looking around the room as if he did not know where he was, or what had happened.

"Father," said Ahlifer face pale from sweat and cold air, still shaking as if at that moment he finally made it out of the drowning waters, "We caught a fish."

Fjorn smiled intently at his awoken son, the innocence radiated from his face right back to his own. Drunkenly Fjorn set his cup of mead on the bedside right next to a lantern.

"Ghosts?" He started while slurring noticeably. "Your sister said you saw ghosts."

Ahlifer wriggled his nose trying to become for focused, slapping his cheeks with both hands, he knew he saw a ghost, but his conscious did not want to deal with it.

"Ghosts? Inga? Where is Inga?" He said.

"Inga isn't here. She went for a walk I suppose."

Ahlifer brought himself back down to his back, still in pain, sore in his torso, as if dozens of boulders had fell to his ribs.

He held his abdomen feeling the tight muscles that rummaged along his bones all tender, in pain. His mind started to race a little more, faster than it usual does. The image of himself, being torn apart, flesh dangling, rotting — he held his eyes tightly as if he saw them right then and there.

Fjorn looked down at his son, seeing the frustration, the fear that rose in him when he asked him about the ghosts. Ghosts were common across the bridge due to the amount of unlawful acts of violence and death.

The village was safe, but the other side of its' border, was not. If it were ghosts that plagued his son's young mind, the Jarl would be the first to know, for the man did not take light measures when hearing about the superstitious encounters.

"You saw ghosts, didn't you?" Asked Fjorn

guzzling down some more mead.

"I did not see a ghost," Ahlifer quietly said turning to his side away from his Father. "Inga lied. I must go back to sleep," voice turning with a crack.

"Damn you, boy! You were under the water for over five minutes. Any mortal man would have drowned. Then your sister says you see some ghosts, last words marked by you as you then lied limp in my arms," Fjorn threw his cup down watching the rest of the mead pour out, just as his patience was. "You are supposed to be dead! Gone! With the Gods, but you lie here as if you merely just tripped over a rock. What ghosts?"

Ahlifer saw his dad become less discerned by the way his eyes unfolded into a glowing light, tears pummeled down his cheeks.

He was scared of that voice replying to his father's own questions, taking charge from here on out, but he remembered, it left as soon as he drowned.

It hurt Ahlifer, more than anything to not be able to reply to his Father's words, but it was for his own good. He wanted to forget the whole situation and move on from it, but he knew the thing he saw was going to haunt him for the rest of his life.

"Fjorn. Your son. What did he see?" Tillu said while rubbing his bearded braids. Dead of night and the man was passed out after a day of hunting boar. He was awoken by the panicking at the docks, rushed by Fjorn to come to his son's aid, now here.
                                        "None of our
worries I do hope," said Fjorn wiping his face trying to sober up. He hadn't had a drink in years, since his wife's passing, now one to cope with the precarious events of his son's sickness, "A ghost of himself or something, I'm not sure. Inga was there. He said so himself," he then finally said.

He walked around the hall to the large fire that illuminated the room with swinging shadows and dim light, he could not sit still, his mind pattering just like the rain outside. His good friend Tillu sat himself down on a bench leaning down towards a bucket of water and began washing his hands gently removing the black stains of charcoal and smoke that lingered from lighting the fire.

Tillu and Fjorn were friends from birth, born on

the same day, and married to their wives on the same day, they were close of friends that they considered themselves kin. Both relied on each other, and called each other brothers even if they were not. He was there when Fjorn's wife passed, a sacred companionship through blood and tears was beyond recognition for the two.

Fjorn stepped back from the fire, eyes still gazing upon the flames trying to imagine the scene of Ahlifer and his doppelgänger staring face to face.

He couldn't think of what sort of magic was responsible for this, but he had heard of this before, people seeing themselves face to face— and then ending up dead weeks later. It's never occurred in their small fishing village though, usually west of there, towards the hills that drew a border along the edges of Rundrej.

"I'm not taking this light," said Fjorn still imagining the burning magical scene.

"And no one should, Fjorn," said back Tillu eyes pressed on his concerned friend, "Sit down, you are making me nervous."

"This is a message. Not a good one either. The God's are telling us something," said Fjorn ignoring his friend. He wasn't superstitious at all, but it was hard to be not when your own son experienced such a thing.

The crack of lightning perfectly sounded the night sky drowning out the village's rain. The flames of the fire spun from a brief, but strong wind.

The room went chill for a second with the shadows moving and flickering. Fjorn looked at Tillu with unease and lowered his eyes. Wind seeped back out of the cracks of the wooden house.

"Whenever a man sees the image of himself, that man is dead," said Fjorn. "But Ahlifer is no man. Just a boy, and a boy with a wild imagination. Can't even tell reality from his mind some of the days."

"Your blood, your sins, brother." replied Tillu still sitting his chair unsure what else to say.

Fjorn nodded in agreement, his head lowered to his chest like a dog knowing he did something wrong. He had to figure out what the future had in store, and when it will be, and how to prevent it, the message was quite clear it was soon.

He knew something terrible was about to happen, for every sign pointed right to it. There were no true answer for his mortal mind. He became still, still as the fire's flames that stood high from the pit.

Ahlifer sat in hid bed curled into a ball staring at his feet, voice still present; though it did not say much, and the presence of it was hard not to ignore.

His ankles, where the invisible chains clasped around showed no signs of that ever happening. The lungs that were full of water were now full of air. His mind though, still uneasy, restless, turning like the oars of a giant kenning, traversing down a narrow river; tight, too tight, it hurt to move the mind, but like any sailor, it must move forward.

Inga walked into the small room hesitantly carrying bread and dried herring for her him. She looked at him in worrisome, regret— she felt it was her fault for what happened to him; her childish actions, her pride had gotten him there. Her Father did not put the blame on her, he put the blame on himself and his cured existence.

"I brought you food," said Inga while setting the plate on his bedside. She saw the water with not even a speck of droplets left in it, he had drank the whole jug. From drinking the whole sea, to drinking a whole jug, her brother was thirsty, "It might help you to remember some stuff."

"I don't want to remember anymore," he quickly said.

Inga lowered her head and let out an irritated sigh, she still kept quiet and patient for her sick brother. She grabbed the plate and started eating it herself. She sat quietly, softly chewing the bread trying not to interrupt her brother's mind.

From being an imaginative boy with dreams that no other person could see to a boy whose imagination were now tormenting.

He was in a perilous cage, a prison—somewhere organically impossible to tread, he wanted out, he did not say it, but he showed it. When no one is in the room, he would try and speak to the voice that put him there, asking for a way out; death was not a choice, for the voice would say to him. No key, no resolution to this madness, no true way out of the lands of eternal madness.

Inga watched for an hour more as her brother

stayed in the same position, hands to the knees, dripping with sweat. He did not spark a fever, nor was he hot, nor cold, but a steady one. Inga had no idea what else to help mend the pain she could not see. She had to figure something out, soon, or the pain would spread to her seeing him that way.

The next day Inga was sitting on the dock where her brother dove in for the fish, she stared into the water, thoughts playing a game of tag, her head spinning. She had her legs in the ocean, ankle deep, bringing in the cold water to her skin. Birds were flying in circles above her in front of the large, and orange sun.

The sounds of the tides hitting the beach full of rocks soothed her mind. Each tide that crashed repressed her thoughts of her brother's unduly health.

The clouds mixed of blues and oranges of color slowly moved to the north, away from the island where she sat perfectly — still distancing herself from the nature that continued on around her. Her shadow rippled along the waves, standing tall on her reflection. She stared angrily at her reflection.

She was annoyed of the innocence that projected into the waves, she did not want to look so weak. She stood up abruptly and started walking towards the inland of her village until Tillu came down on the dock with an ale in hand.

"Where you going?" Slurred Tillu as he watched Inga stomp her way to him with her head down trying to ignore him. She didn't want to be bothered, and instead she wanted to stay in her thoughts.

"To find the white wolf in the forest," she replied still walking past him. She didn't even feel the words come out her mouth. She never even thought of the idea until it came seeping out of her mouth.

Tillu was confused by the 'white wolf' statement, until his drunken mind put it together, the spirit of the island. The legend was that when Odin went back to Valhalla, he kept one of his wolves to protect the people of the island from dangers.

The Wolf then roamed the deep areas of the forests collecting wisdom from the winds that blew in from the distant oceans.

When one is lost,

> *the roads are gone,*
> *the wisdom lies in wait,*
> *In wait in the deep forest,*
> *In wait we wait, we wait.*

Tillu slurred the songs under his breath going back to drinking. He instantly forgot he saw the child go wandering about. The song was to remind them of the Gods, and how they never really left the island. As time grew on, they sang the song, and felt closer to the Wolf that was bound in one with Aesir.

No one ever thought to seek the White Wolf, to the people as they grew, they felt as if it were a myth, a fairytale, and a long forgotten saga. But for the desperate, and stubborn Inga, it was her last resort to find out what had unraveled on her island, and why it picked her brother.

"Good song, a song of something stronger than us," said Tillu trying to remember the last time he had heard that song, he could not, it's been years since the song came out of anyone's mouth, or even the mention of it.

"Well, I was…" Inga started to say trying to think of where she was initially going, she couldn't remember though. The White Wolf wasn't a bad idea, a desperate idea, but a good idea at that. "The White Wolf, I was going to find him." She became even more confused as her mouth did the talking.

"When the roads are gone, wisdom is more bound to sprout from somewhere else," said Tillu again finishing his ale. He gave her a wink and a courteous drunkenly stumble. "Yeah, don't fall in the waters, Tillu. Thanks for the advice," she said making her way towards the West Side of the village towards the forest.

A child's tale, a myth, a frozen remembrance of the past now being picked open in a time where mysteries were sprouting again. She could not figure out why the words came, but so the same as the state of her brother.

The fact Tillu did not hesitate to stop her also was concerning, it was as if a dream was leading the course of reality now and all Inga had to do was to accept it.

<u>**3**</u>

Inga trudged through the thick forest pulling branches for her help to climb through the muddy terrain. The rain didn't help her venture, but it didn't stop her from slowing down.

She loved the nature as much as her brother did. The clan she grew in were about being one with the animals. To fight like a wolf, to parry like a bear, and to die like a boar was the unofficial motto they went by.

Birds hummed and chirped through the silent forest, with branches turning from the wind. She stopped and took in the deep air filled with fresh vegetation, and new life. She watched squirrels run up trees, and bugs crawl on leaves.

She always wondered what it would be like to have been born as an animal, where you were always one with nature, and the priorities of a mortal were nonexistent. She wished she were a bear; sleeping during winter, fishing in the summer, and always being close to their loved ones.

She continued on through the forest, reaching a creak that pleasantly flowed down towards a lake that was approximately two hundred feet away; a good fishing spot where her and her brother would catch fresh pan fish for the adults when they went on raids in the east.

The older people of the village would always come back with shiny, golden treasures that resembled the cultures that went on, and in return Inga and Ahlifer would have fresh fish for them to munch on.

Inga's favorite possession her father brought back was a golden cross they had taken from a place of worship in a small village off the oceans. To her father, it was a worship of some God that defied their Gods. To Inga it was a symbol of discovery and adventure, and broadening of the mind. More Gods than our Gods she always wondered.

She looked past the creak to old statues of worship from the old ones. The old ones were the ones past their generations, and the first inhabitants of their isles.

Two large slippery rocks were bulging out of the little creek for her to climb upon and make herself forward acting as a bridge of some sort. She stepped on the first rock with her right foot feeling it out to see if it were too slippery to pass on. She felt her foot slide a little noticing the slimy moss that stuck to it made it more uneasy for her foot to stay on, so instead she just stubbornly, and hastily walked through the shallow creek. Her boots were full of water by the time she made it to the other side.

She plopped down on a dry rock next to the idols of worship and angrily in annoyance emptied her boots of the water.

"Where in Odin's name is this white wolf?" She asked herself in her head. "I should have planned this more accordingly."

She got up with her now waterless boots on and started up the hill that was covered in trees and more water run offs. The land due to the recent rains made it hard for her, but her being the daughter of Fjorn the Small she had no choice. "The Small" came from Tillu, his closest friend when Fjorn was declined to go on a raid in the West on another small Viking village to reclaim their stolen land.

That's another story for another time, but, they declined him because of his height. Being an adult, fully bearded, but reaching the heights of a boar gave him the name. He snuck on the departing ships and hid in a small enclosed barrel full of fish, hugging his axe tightly until the next day when they arrived to make camp.

Tillu opened the barrel and laughed intensely bringing attention from the other Viking men. They all saw him cuddling an axe and few fish in a barrel, and then given him the nickname "The Small".

Inga dodged the water that ran down the hill by walking on the side sliding from tree to tree. She was running tired, and didn't even think about the time of day it was when she left. The sun was slowly setting which meant only the stars and moon would guide her way.

She grabbed the last tree that covered the hilly and muddy terrain pulling herself up to the flat some-what grassy ground where more trees covered. She never travelled this deep into the forest.

All she knew was the White Wolf was out there some where, and it had answers for what was happening, only if the stories were true, the wolf would answer them all.

She closed in on a lake that covered half of the forest, where old oaks grew out of the water, and rocks were poking out. She looked all around the wooded forest seeing the shadows slowly creeping around as the sun laid down. She needed to find some sort of shelter, or some where dry to start created the lake, and walked to it. It looked old, with muddy blankets, and straw that made up a bed.

She saw rocks circling around that made a small
fire pit with empty tinder completing it. She thought this
was a good place to set up. She grabbed her bag from her
back and swung it to the muddy ground and started to pull
out the necessary items to start a warm fire to shield off the
cold night.

a fire, and make camp.

Her eagerness to help her brother from his
nightmares made it hard to plan accordingly, and instead
she did this all spontaneously which made it harder. Her
willpower did overpower all the other feelings that she
would receive though.

She walked along the lake staring in the cold,
crystal waters watching her reflection walk next to her. She
smiled as if it would make a difference in all of this, but it
didn't, she then sighed bringing her face back to a normal,
emotionless face. She saw an old camp near a waterfall that

<u>3</u>

Ahlifer still stood up in his bed in a trance, dead-like, breathing calmly staring at the fur on the bed that stood up as if it were still connected to the animal. He blinked his eyes every couple of seconds to the dryness that veiled itself over them for when he kept them open too long, staring at nothing.

His eyes, full with dark circles under them, and blotches of red in the whites showed he barely slept. His muscles still tense as if he needed ready his reflexes.

The room was mildly lit by old iron oil lamps that flickered to every air molecule that traveled in its circulation through the room, and also welcoming the new air that travelled through the crack of the bedroom door.

Fjorn left the door open a tad just in case of emergency; whether it be the ghost that tormented his son, or if Ahlifer was about to piss himself of a full bladder. Fjorn was just on the outside of the room sitting quietly in a corner of the room around a circle table and with two axes held on the wall, and a big deer's head mounted in between them right above him.

His friend Tillu straight across of him, and Edvar, his other friend. They were enjoying a midnight's mead, and some smoked fish.

"Are we going huntin' for Inga?" Asked Edvar while he scratched his scarred head in anxious confusion. He worried about these kids as much as the rest due to being close with Fjorn, their father who sat stressed chewing his thumb nervously straight across the table saying nothing back to his question.

Edvar didn't ask it again after that, and instead let his friend stay to himself, despite Edvar's distaste for the quiet atmosphere.

In the next room over, the door quietly closed without either Ahlifer or his father and friends in the next room to notice.

The lamps all sequentially went dark, all beside the one that hovered next to the bed where Ahlifer sat in a profoundly uncomfortable state of mind. The one light that was left circled Ahlifer's body, revealing a moving shadow, tall and long, a man of sorts next to Ahlifer's shadow that sat still on the wall next to the bed.

Ahlifer heard drums beating a terrifying sound in his ears, but paralyzed by fear of his conscience, he stayed still. He felt a cold wind, no, a breath, someone was breathing on his neck as the drum sounds made the horror like sound.

Inga's face flashed in his mind, she was bleeding and moving her lips trying to say something, but mute and emotionless he couldn't figure it out. An image of his father then popped up doing the same thing... bloody, and lips moving at the same rhythm as the drums...

"Are you back?" Asked Ahlifer in his mind hoping to hear the other voice.

The room still stayed steady, the drums stayed steadily sound, he moved his arm to his neck to speculate the air that touched his skin, making his neck hairs stand up. He moved his arm... he was surprised. He quickly laid it back to his side in fear of if something would notice. Silence, rain, drums, breathing, images. Silence, rain, breathing, drums... his sister talking... now his sister is talking to him in his head.

"Yes," said the voice disguised as Inga's. "I went to search for you, and now I'm dead."

Ahlifer's hair's stood up, still hearing the deep sound of drums, and hearing his sister's voice who was supposedly dead talk to her.

The sounds of rain dropping heavily on the wooden roof helped play a role in this organically horrific orchestra that played only for the boy who was frozen, and damned by his mind, and the demon who played at the damaged wiring of his brain as if it were the only stringed instrument.

"I am now dead because of you Ahlifer. I think it's time…" started the voice still disguised as his sister's.

"I think it's time to go."

"To die?" He quickly asked not trying to blink in fear he will see his other self.

"To live. They will die. You will live. You have to do something though for your life."

"What is that?"

"You have to simply kill the Gods," laughed the voice.

Ahlifer pressed his eyes together hoping for the blackness to be the screen for the maddened voice to be portrayed. Inga's eyes, hollow, and full of blood that spilled out gently over her cheek bones with her mouth moving silently. He put the last words the voice had said to him over the mouth, matching it… His father, his sister… the voice… He was now feeling hatred rise through his skin and burn. His hands clenched not in reflex, but from the effects of this burning anger.

"You do feel it. You feel that strength that could kill a God… or two," the voice said now in the voice of Ahlifer's. "You feel like you can, because you could, or vice versa. The God's have given you death and nothing more. You are no longer Ahlifer the Small, a name you were given from your father's past. No, you are Ahlifer the Wicked, the boy, err… man, who killed the Gods!"

"That's pretty impossible," said Ahlifer in a tone of annoyance. He was getting closer to finding out who the voice was, and he knew it wasn't his mind going mad. His anger settled down leaving him a little less rage filled.

"So, I kill your family. Beautiful, beautiful."

<u>**4**</u>

Hungry, yet still happy, unusually Edvar started humming a tune of an old song he'd sing with Fjorn and Tillu when they were on fishing expeditions that would last them from anywhere of seven days to four weeks. The song was about Thor outdrinking any Giant. It was passed down through the sagas. The melodic humming distracted his own racing mind.

"Is that the song I think it is?" Asked Tillu.

"It be tha' one," responded Edvar pausing his melody for the time being. "Now imagine if us' could out drink a bunch of giants of the frost. That'd be a tale to tell."

"Our mortal bellies wouldn't last," laughed Tillu.

Fjorn still sat silently, yet smiling to his two friends laughing over memories and the sagas of the Gods they worshipped. To the men, anyone who could outdrink a giant was a warrior indeed, and to even eat more than one, well, that man was a God. Thor, the God of Thunder in fact did both back in old when they still roamed the Earth.

"Tillu would be drinkin' and I'd be eatin' and Fjorn you'd be… well, most likely doing both, because you are strongest of us lot," loudly laughed Edvar. "In fact, I bet you be Thor. Gold bear, muscles, and the rest. Where you hidin' your hammer?"

Fjorn laughed unintentionally to his friends' joke, or idea- you never knew what was in Edvar's damaged brain.

He lunged himself over the table to his friend speaking madness and grabbed him by the collar of his tunic and looked darkly in his face, "You better not tell a single mortal about my whereabouts and about my hammer, stupid mortal."

They all quieted down intensely after Fjorn slid back to his chair where mead, and ale was dropped upon drenching his bottom in the alcohol he abruptly got up holding his bottom, "God's be proud, I pissed myself!" And with that, they all blasted out of laughing uncontrollably. Fjorn still holding his drenched bottom he went towards the fire still endlessly laughing.

"The almighty Thor bout pissed himself over a damned mortal!" Laughed Edvar.

"Yeah, and you bout to piss yourself when I take my hammer and scorch your head with it for the final blow," responded Fjorn with laughter.

"Praise the Gods! It took a God to finally put a weapon through ol' Edvar's head. Thanks fer' gettin' me a saga of me own."

They all chuckled together drunkenly around the table full of empty horns, and fish heads. The men smiled happily at one another forgetting about the distraught of the curse that had been brought on Fjorn's child.

Edvar slid his meaty hands across the table leaning towards Fjorn's right shoulder and held onto him smiling giving appreciation to his unnecessary friendship, and with that… he slipped belly first onto the table, drunkenly wiggling around on it, sitting himself up.

They laughed even more to the sight of Edvar's shirt caught on the top side of his belly revealing his hair under skin.

"Edvar! Half-man… HALF BEAR!" Shouted Tillu while lifting more of his shirt up revealing his chest full of rough brown hair. "You are the Bronzed Bear! Maybe Inga should have stayed here and see what wisdom this spirit that lies before us has!"

Fjorn looked at Tillu smiling, and turn his lips down into a frown remembering that his daughter was out in the woods alone in search of something he knew was a myth.

He now hated his mind and himself for letting her go out into a dangerous woods, but at the time he needed to stay with Ahlifer.

His mind raced from his annoying thoughts and the alcohol he combined it with. He went limp, and his head dropped to the table sounding a huge *thud* through the whole lodge.

<u>**5**</u>

The woods were cold at the time of night Inga decided to find shelter, but she steeped still under an old oak that curved over her where she draped a large fur coat she found at the campsite prior to make a tent. The fire next to her crackled to the tinder succumbing to the flames, and the winds stayed at peace. She hadn't been sleeping as she had wanted to for the past few days since her brother's untimely incident.

Her stubbornness and sense of adventure led her here, and the curiosity of new worlds tinged her mind causing her mind to precociously turn into desperation.

Her desperation laid hidden deep, deeper than her subconscious which would have told her to not act so foolishly, but wherever this feeling of desperation came, it did not come from her always logical mind; it came from her feeling of love for the ones she did not want to see lost, and the thoughts of her being able to prevent them from being lost. She knew her brother would be forever lost in whatever darkness consumed him, so she took the leap, and sprung into whatever last hope there was.

"Demons, eh?" Said a soothing, yet gauntly voice to the sleeping Inga who was curled into a ball under a dirty tunic that was left at the camp prior to her stay. She twitched in her sleep noticing the voice, but still dreamed of her brother by the docks before his fall.

"Your brother and his demons?" The voice said again, but not to her, but to himself in wonderment. The voice sounded happy for some reason, and Inga couldn't understand, she was in a lucid state of her and her memory, and now a strange voice. Her eyes twitched some more begging her to wake up and see who this figure was.

She awoke quietly, keeping her eyes half way closed. She didn't know if this voice was the same voice that approached her brother, or if it were a bandit of some sorts about to kill her, or do worse, so she stayed quiet, pretending to sleep. Her anxious heart beat picked up tuning out the sound of her racing mind.

"Your heartbeat, the drums of a morning tune. What demons? What brother?" Asked the voice still with a rough, worn out tone.
But Inga didn't respond, and instead turned her back naturally to the voice pretending to be fast asleep. She felt a warm hand touch her shoulder, turning her back to her side. It frightened her, made her panic. Was she going to die? Why was this man so insistent for her to wake up? Why did he keep mentioning her brother? Demons? Why demons? Questions pulsed her thoughts making her heart race.

"No mortal's heart beats so fast when asleep. I know you can hear me. No one can fool a God, especially a God of All-Knowing…" he said making her eyes open swiftly to the last sentence where she cautiously turned herself towards the large man hidden under the moon's shadow. "I do not come here in mortal form, but my own self, this is a serious expedition for me and your innocence I know will not let you say anything to any other mortal… or may it be I am too sloppy when in such desperation."

The clouds moved, so did the shadows over the large bearded man, revealing one eye open, and one eye hidden under a patched leather band that wrapped around long frosted-orange hair that draped back beyond the man's neck. "You know who I am. Now, I must know who you are, and why you are so damned important." Ended the tall, and prominent looking man, who no doubt was no other than Odin, the All-Father, and The God of Never-Ending Wisdom.

<u>6</u>

Edvar and Tillu sat around their friend Fjorn as he laid flat in a bed lifeless. The morning sun shined through harshly, but was covered lightly by two linen drapes. The smell of spices, and seasons flooded the room causing a more peaceful atmosphere for the sick Fjorn. A bucket made of wood and iron clasps sat next to Fjorn's bedside for when he woke and was able to drink. The mess of mead, and ale still lingered around the broken table that Edvar fell on, table legs splintered, and half-way on a thread hanging.

No one remembered the rest of that night. A few too many ales would do that for any common man who had a tendency to overdue their drinking. They staggered around the room with headaches, and grogginess holding their stomachs and sore muscles, all besides Fjorn who laid still still, and barely breathing. This was no ordinary hangover for the man. Like Edvar, and Tillu had previously agreed, if anyone could outdrink anyone, it would be their friend Fjorn. So what was wrong with him? Only the Gods did know.

"I can't help but to think we killed our friend," said Edvar looking pale and sick to Tillu. Tillu ignored him and kept his attention on the one friend he called brother that laid lifeless in front of him. The men felt as if it were their fault, but only Edvar would admit it, for Tillu would deny it openly even if his heart had said different. He was ashamed of what was happening.

The door slid open revealing a tall, pudgy man wearing a bear skin on his back as a cape, and a circlet made of jewels. It was the Jarl of the island, and he looked at the men with an uneasy, yet pleasant face. He shut the door behind him and walked in, closing out the sun light that would kill any man who had drank too many. He approached the bed side to look at Fjorn's face that was only pale, and sweaty.

"I heard word," started The Jarl but was interrupted with a huge sigh he profoundly let out, "I heard word… Fjorn's son and daughter are missing."

Tillu turned his head to the Jarl and confidently nodded disregarding the attempt to say anymore. He didn't know what to tell the Jarl about how mad Fjorn's family was going because he knew deep down there was more to do with it and he also knew the Jarl was superstitiously cautious about such tragedies that he'd exile the three of them off the island immediately.

The night was again hazy for the two friends, and that's why they felt guilty. Ahlifer disappeared from his bed, the same bed they laid Fjorn on, and Inga was known to be in the woods in search of the White Wolf.

The more the two thought about it, maybe they were cursed, but as close as they were with that family, they had to defend them otherwise.

"I think he just drank too much. Gods wouldn't dare touch a man like Fjorn, until he dies in battle," added Edvar trying to ease the situation. He didn't understand why the Jarl was there in the first place, and why would he come alone. He barely knew Fjorn, and he barely knew him and Tillu. Why such a sympathetic act at this time.

The Jarl removed his bear pelt and sat it on a stool in the corner of the room, and kneeled on the side of his bed sliding uncomfortably close to Fjorn's cheek.

Edvar snorted trying to hide his immature laugh from the thought that the Jarl only came here to kiss Fjorn. He covered it up with a synthetic cough and a growl pretending he was still drunk.

He most likely was still drunk, but despite that fact, he didn't want to foolishly laugh at a time like this.

"I only came here in question for where his kids might be," said the Jarl with his head turned still kneeling at Fjorn's side. "It's been a week I hear."

"Two days or so. No week," said Edvar.

"Still, we will have a 'Thing' later this afternoon. Too many people have been saying rumors these little ones are cursed. The girl ran into the woods.

The boy seeing the dead. Now their father in some sort of death-like state barely breathing. Now, that's a sign of upcoming death to us all."

The Jarl was very superstitious and it made him sometimes act irrationally. In the past, if one was sick, he would cast them out to die, or sometimes they lived and joined another clan.

The Jarl went by the name of Ullfr the Mad to some of the men and it was all because of his insane reactions to such little incidents that could be easily prevented. His eyes were always darkened as if he could never sleep because of his mind was always in paranoia. He always led his region, the island with force, and insensitive fear.

The Jarl leaned back up grabbing his bear pelt and slid it back onto his back clasping two strings to the two iron buttons that were sewn onto his tunic. He looked at Tillu and Edvar in a ghostly, and emotionless face and then let himself out with no more words leaving the two friends uneasy.

"Fuck, every time I have met that man on raids, or fishing trips, that man is always looking half dead like he fucked Hel himself," said Edvar shaking.

Tillu started to laugh out loud, and then quickly turning his laugh quieter in fear of Ullfr hearing him. Edvar grabbed the bucket of water and dunked his head into it to make sure he was still sane.

The two then became nervous of what they would say at the 'Thing'. They knew there was a terrible outcome of all this and they knew how they could avoid it, and it was by some how waking up their maybe, most-likely dead friend who laid unconscious on the bed.

<u>7</u>

The woods were softly lit by the morning sun that projected through the canopies of the wet trees. The leaves glistened from the water droplets that interacted with the rays of light, and the waters of the lake stood silently still.

Inga sat cross legged around the dying fire, and across her was Odin. She was still at awe, and yet confusion. She never expected meeting a God in her life time until the end of her life time. The two sat silently eating fish together.

Munching, and wriggling every meat off the bones. This was the closest any mortal would get to feasting with the All-Father, and that gave Inga a sense of self-pride.

"So, demons you said in your sleep, and brother? What did you mean?" Asked Odin putting his fish down on a tin plate turning to the little girl with amber-gold hair that went into two braids to her jaw bones. "My ravens told me this is where I would find what I was looking for."

"What are you looking for?" Asked Inga with no hesitation.

"Loki-."

"Loki!" Exclaimed Inga interestingly.

"Loki escaped, and we are in search of him, and my Ravens have said this is where he has been seen the last. Now, I have wisdom, but you know not as much wisdom as nature does," laughed Odin.

Inga was now reminiscing of the past with her brother at the dock and remembering what had happened, and now she was linking it to the Trickster God's actions and how it all now had connected. She was bewildered, and stunned by her findings. Loki was always good with the Gods and the word *escaped* made it sound like he wasn't, and that's what made her the most curious. Odin looking for Loki. A God hunting for another God, and involving a feeble mortal into it was shocking.

"What did he do?"

"What Loki does best?"

"Tampers with something he shouldn't?"

"Aye. Now leaving another dead."

"Dead? Gods can die?" Asked Inga leaving her head in wonderment with more questions. She wanted to ask him more, but she knew that would be disrespectful, and a little bit rude, especially since Odin was naturally relying on her.

Whatever those Ravens saw pointed Loki in the direction to her island, and that pointed to the connection of Ahlifer's mad mind. He was playing tricks with him, leading him to insanity, but why?

She wanted to ask him that, but she felt it was her mortal obligation to answer his own questions first, before she kept asking hers.

"Everything dies eventually. We are all fragile, and it is the weak spots that will kill us, and Loki knew how to exploit them."

"I never saw Loki," Inga said respectfully going back to his initial question.

"He wouldn't show himself."

"Then how would I know?"

"Your brother, and demons? What did that mean?" Asked Odin sternly with his one eye.

"Ahlifer…" she started draping her head down to her chest, and then quickly back up putting her eyes to his. "My brother.

He's gone mad, and no one knows why. He drowned in the waters fishing. He came back up though after five minutes of staying under. He said he saw himself under there staring back at him, but it wasn't a direct image of himself, but it was him decayed and dead. The voice taunted him."

"Death will be right around the corner, this is his is final joke, he knew he had gone too far, and he knows that we are done with it. Thor is in the East, in Jotunheim, the cold land where giants rule. Tyr is in the West in Alfheim, and I'm here right in the middle…"

"Midgard," said Inga with a cold dead stare into Odin's one eye. She and her people have always called in Earth, but the sagas recognized the land as Midgard. This was a whole different level of perception for the young girl.

Odin slid his bag too the side through the wet brush underneath him. He started to hum a tune that was unrecognizable to Inga.

He pulled out a pipe and filled it with tobacco and lit it from a twig he set ablaze from the resting fire in front of him and his newly founded mortal companion. He inhaled deeply and exhaled smoothly blowing the smoke out in front him into the fire. The fire turned green, then purple, and then back to its normal color.

Inga's eyes widened. She felt a comfort among the fire she hadn't felt before. Odin's one eye closed, and he continued humming the song more loudly.

The winds picked up, leaves twirled around in circles all around them with the fire now standing upright without moving.

Inga couldn't keep her eyes off the pausing embers. The whole world felt as it paused, she felt the world she known was transpiring into a different one.

Odin sat across her with his head tilt down humming that strange tune, and then stopped. The world started moving again, and Inga snapped herself out of the daze she was in.

"What just happened?" Said Inga.
"Wisdom. I have to get it some where."
"The nature?" Asked Inga bright eyed.

Odin nodded.

"I need to go to your village."

"Where do I go?"

"You stay put. The birds will sing a weird tune if you must leave right away, and if and when that happens... you run towards the north side of the creek. You will see a boat there, it's small, and built for two with oars made of green wood, and you take it, do not paddle, and just let the river take you."

"Where will it take me?"

"Questions. Questions. Questions. No more, and just do what I say. You will be safer there."

Inga didn't say anymore in fear of Odin's patience would dissipate, and instead nodded unsurely to his words. For a God to mettle with mortal's destinies is something the sagas did not speak about.

Maybe, this was a new saga for Inga. She felt the world around her slowly die, and she didn't know how she got that feeling. She ignored it, and stayed still watching Odin in a long cape and a wooden walking stick walk toward her home. Her home she knew, her home she knew she wouldn't see again for a long time.

8

Tillu stroked his beard by the docks peering into the waters. He looked out towards the edge of the sea contemplating on how he and Edvar would handle the Thing later in the afternoon. The Thing was held in a longhouse across the little house they kept Fjorn.

It's where the people of the island would gather and diplomatically solve their issues. Some small, and some so big where it would either mean an axe to the neck, or banishment from the region.

Tillu knew how nervously superstitious their Jarl could get, and that lead him to being more volatile, which could cause Fjorn's death, Ahlifer's, and even Inga's. They had to come up with something really fast.

Edvar came walking down the old dock, shaking it as he walked holding two freshly poured ales in two mugs for him and Tillu. The both shared drinks together awaiting the suns special mark in the sky indicating afternoon. Impatiently, and tipsy they stared together into the sun's heat both intoxicated by the ale and the beauty of the nature that surrounded them.

"Beautiful day," said Edvar.

Tillu nodded eyes still fixed to the sun.

"What say we chug these drinks and make our way to the Thing," said Edvar.

"Shall be fun, but I'm going to wait a moment to catch my buzz."

Edvar chuckled, and then let out a little belch and started walking back to the village with his half drunken mug.

He knew it was best to let Tillu do whatever he needed in peace, and he sure didn't want to interrupt his thinking process for it could disrupt their friend's safety. He relied on his friend's logic, because it was something he lacked.

Edvar slowly walked through the village where the Karl's all did their daily duties of cleaning their hunts, building structures, and mingling in the middle around a giant stone well that was used for their water supplies. Two women stared coldly at Edvar, and he being slightly drunk was annoyed by it.

"What ya want?" Said Edvar stopping in front of them.

"Nothing," the woman with long brown hair replied, while her friend with short golden hair continued to drink next to her ignoring the confrontation.

"Sure?"

"We are sure."

Edvar shook his head brashly, sternly smiling them down as he walked away with his next footing shoving himself into an older man half his height. The little old man had a long gray beard and wrinkled that bolted down his forehead, and crows feet the size of an actual crow. He was just missing feathers and a beak, and the old man would have matched perfectly.

"S'cuse me, old timer," said Edvar.

The old man looked up to Edvars double chin and scars under it with displeasure. The old usually were respected in most clans, but not this clan on the fishing village because of their paranoid Jarl who felt as if they were burdens castes onto them for not dying earlier in battles.

They could own houses like any other Karls, but they couldn't do as much more than that. Half of the bounties from hunts were given to the elderly, and a small fraction of wealth as well.

"You're excused," smiled the old man showing his rotted teeth. "They were talking about your friend, Fjorn by the way."

Edvar turned his head back again looking eye to eye down to the older man, "What bout' him?"

"Small talk, really. Son and Daughter. Dead Wife. The normal chatter for a woman that aren't allowed on hunts and raids. Oh, and the upcoming Thing that has to do with their charades."

Edvar looked up to the glowing sun seeing that it had hit it's mark meaning it was afternoon which meant that the Thing was going on now…

Tillu drank slowly, dipping his legs in the water. It was refreshing for him, he was in the stables all day, he saw the muck of horse manure and dirt was away. He didn't want to go to the Thing, so he stayed out by the docks, it was peaceful. Irresponsible and disrespectful, he knew, but he couldn't bare himself to hear the accusations and the outcomes of his dear friend, his brother. Inevitably it would lead to death, or exile, but most likely a painful death. So he drank peering off into the ocean with only his mind.

The ocean tides slowly rippled in shining the afternoon's sun, glittering, and warming. Tillu was becoming more intoxicated by the beauty that surrounded him, and mostly from the alcohol that he kept consuming. When things were out of his hands, he'd drink to it, and pray the Gods would help do something about it.

Unlike Edvar who faced the battles head on telling the stories from the scars on his head. If Fjorn was conscience, he would slap Tillu and tell him the same thing he always says, "Move on with it, Tillu! Booze will only slow your mind, and it is meant for celebration, and until the battle has been won, is when we drink!" It was a hypocritical saying, Fjorn also was accustomed to the booze when life gave him too much to handle.

Fjorn faced many travesties in life, and a rugged path way he walked not alone, but with his friends and remaining children.

His wife, for instance who died from an illness that killed her. Bed sicken for weeks on weeks, and sleeping for half of it, she died peacefully in her sleep. It killed him, and it killed Ahlifer.

Inga was just a little girl learning to walk and talk at the time, and had no recollection of her mother, but Ahlifer did, and he always told Inga she had her nose, and that always brought Fjorn to tears.

Rough and rugged, Fjorn had emotions that he couldn't hide at times, and he always felt vulnerable when they were triggered. His friends sought to help him through and through, and to bring back his strength and courage when he had none.

Tillu imagined Fjorn on his bed, lying lifeless, cold-blooded than he already was dripping in sweat. He wanted to help him as usual, even if it was out of his hands. Curing illness was a Vanir's job, only if they wanted it to be done. He hoped he didn't die, or be exiled, he wanted his friend to at least die in battle so he can forever drink with Odin and the rest, but he knew that wouldn't happen if this Thing had been brought to place- especially by a not so sane man, The Jarl who sought only out power, and to be relatable to the Gods. The problem with Ullfr was that he wanted to be a God, and not just any God, but the God who calls it all, and makes the decisions of humanity, and that was his weak point because he wasn't a God… He was only a man with a mere sickness called pride that furnaced his ego.

> *"The sun is set in the middle of Hel,*
> *Where no human is able to dwell,*
> *Why the sun you ask?*
> *Why the sun, and why it basks,*
> *In the middle of Hel.*
> *In the middle of Hel."*

Tillu raised his mead to the sunny sky. Death by no defeat would give Fjorn an eternity in Hel until the horns blew and the caws of the birds sounded. He loved singing that song, but right now, it hit too close to home for him.

If chugging some of his extra ale he kept in his canteen, emptying the rest into the sea. His eyes were glossy from tears, and drunkenness. He slowly pushed himself up from the dock still barefooted, and started walking towards the village.

"You helped me, and now I'll help you, friend," he said under his breath to himself.

$\underline{\underline{9}}$

People coldly clambered around; farmers, fishers, drunks, they all stayed quiet, sharply awaiting for the Jarl to speak. The Jarl stood on a raised wooden platform in the middle of the lodge. His hair finely done laying down on the back of his cloak made of bear hide, he instructed a man to come to the podium without haste. He wanted this done.

"The man is sick from his wife's death, and so are his children," the man started to say. "I don't think death would do justice for the God's. I think the least we need in this village is more of our people's lives put to death for superstitions without out any evidence to back up."

The Jarl stayed quiet, blindly following every word of it even though his own people wanted something different than he already had set.

"So we sit, and wait, until it leads in a circle where everyone is cursed by the Gods," Jarl Ullfr spoke coldly, his superstitions getting the best of him once again, "No, I won't stand by while my people die out from the Gods neglect. They are mad, and so they should be! You have given up on them and they send this plague as a curse to us all."

"Showing us what?" Asked a man in a long traveling cloak with a walking stick his hood covering his eyes only showing his long greying beard. "What are the Gods showing us, Jarl?"

"They are showing them what its like to live with disobedience towards their own leader!" Choked the Jarl now nerved, he was never used to being challenged. He did not even know the man, "A traveler has no say in another villages matters. Who are you?"

The gray beard only showing, eyes still covered, the Old Man kept pressing for answers, subtly interrogating the Jarl's own pride, his strength now a weakness.

The crowds of the folk who attended the Thing were in awe by this Old Man — his rebellious nature for being a man outside the lands, speaking as if he knew the Jarl. They muttered words among themselves.

Edvar was in the back of the room, behind the crowd. His trusty weapon of mead in one hand, and the other stroking his beard. He felt as if he knew the Old Man, something familiar stood out about him.

The door creaked open right behind Edvar, opening it stood Tillu. He quietly, stumbling over to his bald friend. He put one hand to gain his balance on the shoulder of another who stood on the other side. He used multiple shoulders of people to climb his way towards Edvar.

"Tillu."

"Edvar," Tillu almost fell down but he quickly grabbed onto Edvar's shoulder, "Found me way."

"Where were you?" He smelled the mead that fumed off of his friend's facial hair. His breath was steaming with the stuff.

"Thinking as usual."

The two said no more and looked back at the the old man and the Jarl arguing amongst each other. They were both delighted. Tillu was the most. It put his mind at ease when he saw a passerby standing up for his own friend when his voice alone would do nothing at all.

"I have more a'say than most folk here," countered the Old Man back at the Jarl, "What happened to him is not a curse by the Gods, but a God. Do you know of the stories?"

"How do you say this without evidence?" Asked the Jarl ignoring the man's questions.

"How do you punish an ill man without evidence assuming he is a curse from the Gods?"

Silence.

Ullfr turned away from the man, in contempt with the Old Man's words. He wanted this man out of his village. His anger only rising more, his chest pounding like the war drums that were sounded years ago. He turned back to the other man who first spoke, "So, you think we need to accept the curse? This plague?"

"I do not know," the man stumbled, he did not know if he was speaking out of turn, scared of the Jarl's increasing temper. He knew if he said the wrong thing, it would be his head, his back split open along with Fjorn's.

Everyone in the Thing were all dark, from the shadows and the tone of Ullfr's high tempered voice. They looked back at the Old Man still standing boldly and unwavering. They talked of the beard, his appearance, how strange it was, and how seemingly familiar it was.

The Old Man approached the podium, still not letting down his wits. He was more irate the more the Jarl kept his smug, prideful posture. He saw the blue in his eyes, the flames that kindled beneath it. An odd symbol deep within his pupil. The Old Man did not like it.

"What made them go mad do you think?" Whispered Odin into his ear. He felt the flames roar, he heard the screams of Hel, "You will tell me now." He leaned back to the crowd's around them.

"We just know the boy went mad, and his father fell through right after with him but into a deep sleep of unconsciousness."

"What happened to the boy?" Odin held tight to the man's pride being defeated. Not all enemies were visible, especially the true Ullfr.

"He saw demons, and his own flesh be ripped from him. He is gone now and missing," sneered the Jarl moving back from Odin quickly turning his attention back to the crowd.

"You know who I am, that is why you cower right now," The Old Man held his tongue before he said too much.

"Odin, yes," the Jarl came back to now the Old Man's ear. "The one who makes the choices, the one who rejects the dead who are not pierced, scoured in battle. We know you, and we will fight your warriors soon," he stopped, licking his lips, turning back to the people that circled the small oak podium. His sly, vile, poisonous look turned into the one of a confident, stoic one.

Odin was displeased with the course he took, but he had to excuse himself quickly away back into the village commons. He knew nothing good was going to come out of this, this is what Loki caused, this is what Loki wanted.

He had to stay one step ahead of his enemy, he needed to visit the boy's father who stayed far away from his own trial.

Loki was in hiding, and using this boy as an escape to get out of it. Deceitful, tricky, yet persuasive— it fueled a fire far bigger than any of the other Aesir could kindle themselves.

"Following me?" Asked Odin to the bald man behind him rustling in the berry bushes. He saw him since he left the Thing, secretly maneuvering between boxes of fish and fruit, the well of granite that stood in front of the

Lodge and then to where he finally caught on, right by a bush in front of Fjorn's own house.

"No, just going to the pisser. A man's gots ta' piss when these things take for long," The bald man was Edvar of course. The only bald headed man of middle age in the whole village, "You being an ol' man, you know when you got'sta go, aye?" He was nervous, but he kept his composure just fine—except he was talking to the All-Father himself. Any other man, he would have been able to talk his way through.

"You were barely in there," retorted Odin pulling out his pipe of golden runes, carefully filling it with tobacco.

"Too much ale before hand. Held it in too long since I be started drinkin'," Edvar pretended to unlatch is belt, "You know how that is, aye? Lots of drinkin' Lots of Pissin'," He could not go on demand which made him more nervous. His ploy gone wrong.

"Always room for more, aye?" Smiled Odin lighting his pipe with a twig. He briskly threw it in the copper torch head that kept its flame.

"What you drinkin'?" His eyes wide by the fact a stranger, not from his own village was offering the drunken loaf a free drink.

Odin paused to the question and started digging in his bag retrieving a golden canteen jug of his own. The gold flashed the drunk's eyes, "Gold..." his eyes still affixed to the canteen. Gold! Nothing more caught his own attention, not even the runes that burned on the seals of the leather canvas that wrapped around it, no, it was the gold—a human's weakness, instantly forgetting about the many ales he had before.

"Aye, gold. Have your drink, brother."

"You must be from higher up Steinsgaard," Edvar said back reaching out for the golden canteen, "Tor is more with iron, copper, and the likes," he took a sniff of the brew inside the canteen, measuring the amount he could consume. He usually did this to see how big of a swig he could handle. It smelled of cherries and honey. He loved that combination.

"Special mead. A gift from the Gods they say," Odin winked to the curious Edvar sniffing and smelling. The aroma was strong, it pierced Edvar's nostrils. Odin saw it, chuckled to himself.

Edvar pulled his head back, letting in the flavors of the honey mead drench his tongue and throat. He replied with a huge cough. His eyes blotched with red drunkenness. A smile plucked his lips.

"Have it," Odin said emptying out the ash of his pipe, "It's a celebration and gift for us," Odin took the mead back having a sip for himself, and then raising it high above him to the cloudy sky, "Skål!"

"Skål!" Cheered Edvar with an exciting sway. He was drunk again. This time it felt good, a sober thought or two could pass him without being mixed up on his tongue when trying to speak.

"Brewed from the Giants they say," he was putting the mead back into his knapsack, "Made of special ingredients, brewed in special pots under fires that would never die," Odin looked back up to his new friend, "Where is Fjorn?"

"Over here. Follow me," said Edvar without discourse. He could not hold his tongue nor his thoughts any more. He did what the Stranger said without questioning. He felt overwhelmed with emotions of the newly founded love of companionship. He felt as if he was friends, brothers with this man the entire time. Being Odin, he was, but it was a different puzzle that was figuring itself out now for him.

The two walked towards the little lodge where Fjorn was laying still peacefully out cold on his straw bed full of animal hides covering him. Odin peered down to the mortal man's pale, sweaty face in intrigue. He knew the man was dying, but from what was the question. Was this to do with Loki's actions and the boy he had abducted? Odin had to find out more while the Thing was still in session so it didn't draw too much suspicion. Edvar took another sip of the golden jug full of mead and growled in satisfaction as the strong, and thick liquid washed down his throat.

"This be him," Edvar said too infatuated with the liquid out of the golden canteen. He kept his sights on the burning runes now.

"How long has he been like this?" Asked Odin.

"Since last night."

"What happened?"

"Drank too much I was assuming at first, but, he didn't wake up since, and then the Jarl was came, and now we have a Thing goin'," said Edvar words in a bunch, still affixed to the runes, trying to solve what they meant or what they said.

Odin bent down setting his belongings to the side of the bed. He took his fingers still wrapped in cloth, hiding his tattooed hands, striding them over the man's cold dead face. The cloths unfurled into bands of bandages that he tossed to the side. He pried open Fjorn's eyes to look deeper into them. He jolted back closing them once again.

"What?" Asked Edvar as he saw Odin's mouth drop into a natural frown. "What's wrong?" Edvar threw the mead to the side. He ran to his friend's side next to Odin's.

"You're friend has no sight anymore, he has no pupils to show him this living world. He has gone to the other side. Not dead, nor living," he licked his dried lips, "Helheim. The Goddess is pulling him there with the help of someone else," Odin was saying too much, but he had no choice. If Edvar didn't drink the mead, he would have been able to take it all in. Remember this, be able to adjust to these new words.

"Are you some sort of seer?" Edvar asked scratching his itchy scarred head. He was trying to keep his balance from the swaying caused by the odd thoughts he was having, "What am I even thinking right now?" Edvar felt as if he should have been more concerned, sadder from the sights of his dying friend, the dark words of Helheim, the Gods, but he could only feel his wits still at bay.

His face all smug, grim, full of curious yet dilute colors. He ignored the balder man's questions and kept his focus and studies on Fjorn. He saw the Gebo in his eyes. Burning blind in the corner of his whites. Red fires washed away the pupils. Odin knew who caused this, but he could say no more to his mortal friend.

"Your friend won't come out of this," said Odin. "I'm taking him."

"Well, can you fix him?"

"I can fix him, when is this Thing supposed to be done?"

"Soon I'm sure," as soon as Edvar said that, he heard the large wooden doors of the Thing's Lodge burst open with people pouring out. The chatters were coming closer, everyone was soon to disperse back to their homes and jobs.

Without haste, Odin picked up the unconscious man, scooping him up on his shoulder. With one arm on Fjorn's waist holding him tight, the other grabbing his knapsack, which he slung around his open shoulder.

He paused as soon as he saw the front door inches between him to the sound of Edvar coughing for attention. He turned to the bald man who was now lying on his friend's bed, still drunk, yet at peace, "What do I say when they ask where he went?" He turned on his belly, dropping his arms to the ground, looking like a sloth trying to fly.

"Tell him he went for a walk."

"When he comes back?" Edvar burped, "I mean what will they say when he don't come back?" He burped again rolling back on his back. He was feeling everything, the world tickled him, poked him with unrelenting euphoria.

Odin opened his knapsack grabbing the golden canteen of mead. He threw it to Edvar who was comfortably clawing at the ceiling from the bed. The canteen bounced on the bed which made the bald man laugh with giddiness. He uncorked the cap and drank some more. He felt the coolness melt his witless thinking.

"Fack!" He burped aloud, "Good shite. Keeps you going," he laughed now sitting up. His senses he needed were returning, "I saw some weird shite. Demons of fire and Draugr came crawling their way through the cracks of the ceiling."

Odin stopped his course again, returning to Edvar, "Demons with fire, you said?" He instantly thought of Surtr, the fire giant and his leagues of fiery giants, dogs, and demons, "Anything else?"

Edvar looked up from the bed to the bearded man who still stood high above him. He turned his head lower to remember what else he saw, "a bunch of squirrels with axes and shite too? Lots of colors, some weird beast telling me how to fly above, it all happened so quickly," Edvar drank more after that. He had never had such mead to make him hallucinate, especially when sobering, "Fjorn will be okay, right?" He put the cork back into the top.

"I do not know," he said back apologetically, "Stay calm and keep your wits at the coasts," Odin went back to the door again opening it, "You need to leave, I have done too much here, you're Jarl will come for you," Odin opened the door and left leaving Edvar wide eyed, now attuned to a new fear.

<u>10</u>

Willows, untouched oak trees circled the lake. Inga sat on a rock larger than her, she threw rocks, skipping them through the clear waters. Everything was untouched out in that part of the forest.

Men were too scared to travel, hunt, and fish in fear of the unknown myths — the Draugrs who roamed searching for death, the ogres who relished and fed upon boars, and the spirits of Odin's Wolves.

The sun was setting. Sparkling and flashing through the canopies of the tall trees, hitting her eyes, she squinted at every light that hit her pupils. She saw out into the deep waters, the rocks that skipped to the other side, the banks of tall moss and algae that collected her rocks.

She wriggled her nose to the stone she threw in, the water hitting her nose. She watched it sink. It reminded her of her brother — sinking, to the muddy deep waters, the dark swallowing it from the light, him from the light. She missed him.

Growing up, when their father went off on his own adventures, they would both sit by the dock, talking of life's trials.

They warmed each other bringing hope to another when they felt out of place, alone. No mother to go to, and at times like those, no father. They only had one another.

Over the years, they grew apart. Distancing themselves when they found themselves. Inga being too stubborn, too headstrong, she did not equal out to her brother; who was too lost in his own head, imagining the unimaginable.

Different lands swept his mind turning his own world into a different one. She envied him for that. She always wanted to escape her own.

The sun was set, she saw stones make a bridge of some sort into the middle of the water and her being curious and damned by boredom, she thought it would be interesting to see what it led to.

She knew it was unsafe for the rocks were covered in moss that turned into a slimy repellent for someone to traverse upon. Her natural curiosity deterred the consequences, so she started making her way around the lake to the first rock that would bring her out to the middle.

She cleared the first landing onto the rock without getting wet. Now was the second which was little farther for her reach, and she knew if she missed, she'd be knee deep in water.

She stood carefully eyeing down her target, and she crouched lower for a higher distance, and released, giving herself to the air and clearing the next rock. She was finally content.

Each rock she made, gave her a rewarding satisfaction. She looked beneath her, standing tall looking down into the water, seeing her reflection, her braids that fell down to her neck, her blonde-amber hair, that shined through the remaining light, and her nose… the nose that reminded her family, and her mother. She spaced out.

"Pretty tall," said a squeaky unfamiliar voice.

Inga looked around her seeing no one there, immediately thinking the voice that visited her brother, had come to her.

She paid no attention to it, and instead crouched again ready to make her next jump. She was getting closer to the middle of the lake which meant deeper water.

"I said you're pretty tall!" Said the voice again. It came up above, echoing in the canopies, lowering itself to the rock behind her

She turned around, seeing a little squirrel perched upon the rock she was just on. She thought she was going mad when she saw the little rodent.

She ignored it again looking back towards the rock she was about to jump to. She went in her stance, crouched, and made the jump onto the next one. She breathed heavily due to each jump becoming harder and harder.

"Just like life. Make one jump, you got another one. Obstacles," again said the voice, "Some wise words the bearded one says."

She was infuriated by the annoying words of whatever it was. She turned around again and saw the same little squirrel perched closer to her. She now knew she was going mad.

"Are you talking to me?" Asked Inga to the little squirrel on the stone behind her. She felt weird asking an animal such a question. She felt as if she was losing her mind, or the voice that drowned her brother was now after her. Superstitions plagued her.

The squirrel just twitched its' head in curiosity at the human and shuttered its nose and jumped away towards land and ran up a tree. With everything going on in her life, she could fathom the idea of of animals talking to her. She still shook it off, unapologetically shaking the insanity away.

She focused towards the next rock that sat farther away from her way. She had her doubts on this one, she knew this stone was a little too much for her, but she proceeded to crouch down for her longest jump yet.

She took a deep breath, closing her eyes to calm her mind, and then opened them and sprang high into the air reaching her right foot onto the rock, slipping quickly into the water, splitting her legs, one still on the rock and the other in the water, she fell in.

The water was cold. Her skin bumpy from the icy water. She swam back to the rock she missed, determined to at least touch it. She pulled herself out, damp and drenched. She sat herself on the mossy rock irritated by her defeat.

"Why are you jumping rocks?" Asked the voice once again. "Come climb the trees. More fun."

Now she knew that it was the squirrel. When she saw the little guy run up in the trees towards land, she looked all over the canopy of the forest above her trying to sight him.

"A talking squirrel? You have to be kidding me," she said under her breath in disbelief, wringing out the water that held in her hair.

"Not just any talking squirrel, but one who knows so much. Probably more than your buddy, Odin from earlier," the Squirrel started to chirp, "I like to think of myself as an all knowing, omniscient rodent. Not a God, but I'm working on it," his voice echoed.

"What are you talking about?" She asked looking around up in the canopies. She was more confused and annoyed by this rodent. If it were him, or not, "A squirrel," she let out a sigh, "A damn squirrel. Where are you, rodent?"

"Rodent is a bit harsh, lady," he echoed back, his voice a little more irritated, "I'm not just a squirrel…"

"Okay, where are you?" Inga was more irritated by this mocking creature. She looked all around behind her and kept seeing nothing.

"Up above you!" He laughed.

She looked all around up above her eyeing down each single tree branch that was up there in belief that it was actually a squirrel, and not just her imagination that was always playing games with her as of late.

She felt unbalanced on the rocks when raising her head so she carefully started to sit down when the little squirrel came from behind to jump on her shoulder causing her to jump in the deep water in a natural reflex.

"Why would you jump in the water? It's colder than Ymir's balls in there."

She was treading water looking up to the squirrel who now was on the rock she was supposed to be on. She was soaked, and dripping and shivering from the cold, and also very angry at the little guy who scared her into the water.

"A talking squirrel."

"Like I said, like no other," he chirped back to her.

"I was nearly to that next rock," she said in frustration.

"Nothing is it out there anyway. Why are you jumping rocks?"

"I'm bored," she said.

Inga started swimming back to the shore. The little squirrel jumping along each of the rocks next to her. She pulled herself out, grabbing the edge of some vines that sunk from the shore, dripping and angry.

The squirrel still stayed on the second rock out in fear she would take out her own failures on him. The squirrel knew he was annoying. He had a precocious way of it—his actions and reactions.

Inga went back to the small camp she had scrounged together the previously night. She started to light a fire in hopes she could dry off for when she got the signal to leave.

She still had no clue when and where to go, or when the right time to go was, and now she was talking to animals. Was this Odin's plan?

She huddled closely to the fire warming up staring down her new furry friend. He sat blankly on top of a rusted shovel's handle wriggling his nose.

"Who are you? Do you have a name?" She asked not knowing if animals had names. She didn't know what to talk about with a squirrel, let alone a talking squirrel who always had some sort of profane response.

"Who are you?" The little squirrel quickly countered.

"Inga. Who are you?"

"Nice to meet you, Inga."

"What's your name?"

He blankly stared back, wriggling his nose.

"Do you have a name?" She asked frustratingly. She didn't care if he had a name or not, she just was impatient and this seemed to be the only way to pass time.

"Ratatoskr."

"Your name is Ratatoskr? Like the little gossiping shit in the stories?" Asked Inga with a whimsical tone.

She was in disbelief and in shock that the old stories are coming to life right before her. First Odin which was the most spectacular event that crossed her, and now the little Ratatoskr.

"Yes, that little shit…" he said smiling gruffly, "So, that's how you guys know me? As a little annoying furry ass who annoys the living shit out of everything?"

"No," she quickly replied, "I didn't mean it like that!"

"Really? Then what did you mean?" He was loving every second of it. He was playing with her, just as he did with everything and everyone.

Inga brushed her hair back, drying it a little more by the fire. She didn't know what to say back to the squirrel. She didn't know why he was here. She had to dig deeper and get something out of this chatty fella.

"Ignore it. Why are you in my woods?" She asked.

Ratatoskr hopped closer to her around the fire sniffing the air as he went; catching the scents of burnt pine cones, seeds, and oak. He was always on the hunt for some fresh acorns so he always kept his senses up. He hopped up on her shoulder sniffing higher up in the air.

"Don't ignore me!" She said swatting at him.

"Ignore you? Am I?" He hopped into her lap.

"Why are you in my woods?"

"These aren't your woods. No one can own woods," he snarked back turning away from the questions she kept peppering him with, "How can you own woods?"

"I don't own these woods."

"You said *My Woods* as if they were yours though," he laughed mockingly.

She was more annoyed by him, how he pranced around every question she asked. She hated the sarcastic replies she kept getting from him. She wanted to get something out of him before she had to leave. She didn't know what else to do which caused her nerves to tangle up.

She sat up from the fire, Ratatoskr now back on her shoulder, his nose up in the air still sniffing for food. She grabbed him with one hand, gripping his whole body gently, eyeing him down face to face. She wanted to give the little rodent some kind of fear.

"Why are you in these woods?" She asked.

"Oh. I don't know. Food perhaps? Answers? Intel? I'm always on the go. Some how I ended up here, and then while I was hunting for some nuts, I saw you talking to the Ol' Wise One, Odin, and then immediately had to gather the details of why an Aesir was here talking to a human, and a little girl one at that. Why are you here?" He sat comfortably in her hands knowing she was incapable of hurting something that talked back.

Inga paused at that questions trying to reflect on why she was out in the woods so deep away from her home. She remembered she was searching for the White Wolf, but completely forgot due to the fact she instead found Odin, or he found her, whichever way. She set Ratatoskr down near a log by the fire. She didn't know how to respond to that question. Why was she still out there when she could be at home with her father and Ahlifer? Instead she was now stuck under the command of Odin.

She sat back down next to the stump grabbing her chin in contemplation ignoring the question for now, such as Ratatoskr did with her questions. She remembered Odin saying Loki had to be behind all these unfortunate events around her village, and maybe Ratatoskr would know something about it.

He always is up with the latest gossip. She didn't know if he would, or if he would even be up to answering such questions, but it was her last line to getting to the bottom of this.

"I'm here looking for Loki."

"Loki?!" Jumped Ratatoskr in interest to her response, "See, now I may be a piece of shit, but that man…." He breathed in deeply, and out, bellowing, "He is a bigger piece of shit,"

"Yes, that is what Odin kind of insinuated."

"Why? That guy is hard to keep track of. You're a human anyways. Why would he be here?" He stopped to think, "Ah! Why would he NOT be here? Maybe that's the question," he talked to himself.

"Why are you here? Why is Odin here?" She responded, "Why? Why? Why?" she didn't know why, she just was just irritated on how many turns in her journey had come up.

Her new friend was now the target of the sarcastic, snarky replies. He didn't like it. He hopped quickly back in her lap, staring up to her with his eyes half shut with sympathy for not being fully truthful to her in the beginning.

"Okay."

"Okay?" She said.

"Okay, I'm here… I'm here because I was following Odin from the Tree. I was wondering why in the world an Aesir would go to Midghard, err, Earth. Or whatever. I wanted to know where he was going so I followed him here. Also, I love me some Midgardian nuts from time to time," he started. "From what I've found out from this mystery, is that war is coming here."

"War?!" She said in surprise. "What do you mean war?"

"Like death and stuff. War is coming. Loki is causing it. He wants an army," he sniffed again thinking of the nuts, "He is trying to find some sort of memory, a path to the future," he wriggled his nose again, "Sounds crazy."

"An army for what?" She asked trying to pry more answers out of him. She knew he knew more, if he did, she had to open that little rodent's brain up—by playing with him right back.

Ratatoskr was less hasty on repelling her questions though. Once he got talking, he wouldn't stop. He lived for gossip, chatter, and for answers of what everything was doing in the worlds. Now gossiping with a human girl was his dream, and now its reality.

"Yes! War," he said with certainty, scratching his belly, "Between your people and some other people on another land south of your island. He's got everyone riled up. He knows how to get his way. They are well on there way here too. All I know is that he's gone now."

Inga was overwhelmed with such news. She didn't know how to respond. Her heart felt like it was anchored down, chained, pulling deeper and deeper.

She started packing things from the camp scavenging items that could be of use for her when she got out of the woods and into the creek where she made her escape. She didn't want to now wait for the sign to go, if there was one, she had to act now.

"Where you going?" He was curious when he saw her frigidly leave, no more words, just straight further into the woods. He hopped along with her.

"I need to go to the creek," she was walking to the brush that bordered the tall oaks, moving tree branches and thistles out of her way, back to her camp.

"Why?"

"I just have to."

"I'll come with."

Inga didn't want to argue with the little Ratatoskr anymore, and maybe she could find value in their newly founded relationship. He knew a lot, and she knew too little, and that could help.

She packed an old bag that was left by a barrel with an old fur blanket, and some stones that could be used to start a fire for the future. She grabbed an old lantern that was behind a large boulder and attached it to a long walking stick, and attached them together with some old vines.

She started to walk forward along the lake onto a path that would bring her some what closer to her destination of sanctity.

Ratatoskr followed along oblivious to the emotions that burdened her, and hopped along cheerfully still sniffing for those hidden nuts that dwelled in the forest. He didn't know where he was going, but if she asked, he probably would, but Inga was too overwhelmed to think of even asking that question to him, and so they walked down the old path.

Old runes littered the sides of the path each telling a different story of the ones that were lost in there. She didn't know what they said, and neither did Ratatoskr.

11

The Jarl walked with two of guards attired in fur drabs. They were going towards the little cottage that Fjorn rested in. They were in a hurry, not stopping, marching together through the rain splattered roads.

His pudgy face pale and death-like illuminated through the bright village. His sickness of paranoia of the Gods slowly killing him, and the long attempts at being held higher than a God was piercing his ego.

He only called Things together for his people to feel like they had a say in it, but he always chose for himself before them, and continued to carry out his beliefs even when they were done. He was going to kill Fjorn himself to banish the thoughts of curses along with him.

He was greeted by Edvar at the door, he was still drinking the mead Odin had given him earlier. He was singing songs he had never sang before, or even heard. The mead of song really did him in, and he felt like Bragi, The God of Song himself; swaying back and forth ceremoniously with the gold jug in his hand, he smiled to the bright sky.

> *Oh! Hey, a mortal.*
> *Oh! Hey, a king.*
> *Both the same alike.*
> *Both the same kin.*
> *Blood both covers them,*
> *Taking burdens on,*
> *While meaningful servitude*
> *Sure sings on!*

He ended his song when he saw the Jarl staring into his eyes. Edvar was drunk, but thanks to the magical mead he had been drinking, he could still respond and have full comprehension of his actions and words—a prose too precocious even for him.

"We have come to the conclusion of quiet execution. Bring me to Fjorn," said the Jarl. "I am deeply sorry," he tried to show some artificial sympathy to pry the bald drunk away from the door.

"No can do," laughed Edvar. "My friend awoke from his sleep, and decided to go for a walk."

"A walk?" The Jarl was startled by those words. The flames in his eyes growing, "I don't believe this. Where did he go?" He knew the intentions of Edvar trying to cover for his friend, he knew how most honorable men kept themselves.

"Woods prolly' to find his girl, and his boy," stupidly said Edvar pulling back more mead. He let out a big burp.

The Jarl wasn't taking Edvar's intoxicated replies to light, so he ignored the drunk, signaling his guards to walk with him towards his lodge. He was angrier now that things were out of his control and wanted to kill Fjorn to end the madness upon his village. He stopped by a little house made of straw and granite, and forced himself in without knocking.

The house was Fjorn's; where he raised his wife and kids, where his wife left her final breath. Ullfr was on a rampage, he threw himself in, doors swinging widely in, churning the hinges.

Nothing, no one. The drunk friend spoke true. He became irritated. He sent his burly guards forward through the empty space, having them tear apart family remnants, breaking furniture, stoves that were used for blacksmithing, and everything else that would cause a commotion, hoping to lure the blind man out.

He lit up small kindling in the stoves, feeding larger wood and coal into them. Once the flames were at a respectable height, he lit a torch and had his guards share the flame, starting aflame the interior.

The hot scorches, and heavy smoke killing everything inside; the flowers, plants withering, and insects dropped an scurried to the corners of air. They hoped to smoke the blind man out from the crevasses, the holes, the empty rooms, wherever he may have been hiding. He wanted Fjorn dead. The flames beheld his mind,

Smoke burrowed and twirled in the house. Flames high, crawling up the wooden walls, capturing the ceilings. The wood creaked, cracked, breaking. The Jarl, with dead, cold eyes, still burning blue watched in the middle of the room where Fjorn had his tools.

His guards rushed out, coughing, choking from the smoke that still hung in their lungs. One puking up vile black, the other wiping his eyes, washing them out of a nearby bucket that collected rain water.

"This isn't right," said one wiping his mouth from the vomit that stuck to his beard, "The Jarl is mad."

The other guard put the bucket down, wiping the remaining water on his legs. He was concerned, nervous on what they did. How far they went with the command. He nodded, "This is not what I wanted."

They both knew they blindly followed someone. They worried what that said about their own honor, their own wits. They knew the Gods would not be happy.

Panting heavily, the man held his belly trying to catch the breath he needed in his lungs. He slammed on the locked door to Edvar's house. The door creaked open to the bald man rubbing his head, letting his friend in.

"Fjorn's house is gone," said Tillu quickly, slowly catching his breath. He bent to his knees closing the door behind him.

"Aye, I know," Edvar responded, "I saw them go in. I left when I saw the smoke poking through the walls," he turned his head to his door making sure it was shut tightly.

"You did nothing?" Tillu rose from his knees looking angry into Edvar's dark green eyes, "You just let them in?" He locked the door behind him, "You been drinking all day again?"

"Like always yes, but…"

"But what?"

"You prolly' gon' think I'm more mad than the Jarl when I say this, but I met a strange man," he curled his lips widening his eyes, "Remember the traveler at the Thing today?"

His friend nodded, hoping he'd skip right to the point. He knew he should not be calling out a friend about drinking all day, when he does the same. If anyone should be calling anyone out, it was Fjorn. They both knew that.

"Well, he said some odd stuff," Edvar curled his lips again, "Parently' we supposed to be runnin' from this mean ol' Jarl. Man is on a war path, err, somethin'?"

Tillu walked to one of the chairs where empty jugs and horns sprawled up. He threw them off the chair and surrounding tables, "That's a given," he wanted his friend to continue on. Some times Edvar wasn't the best when speaking words. He gave him the benefit of that doubt.

"War Path," he spoke slowly. He put his stubby finger on his hairy chin, "Wait, I mean… Jarl is coming for us next."

"Where is Fjorn now?" Immediately Tillu said, "Did he burn in his house?" That was what he was trying to get to the entire time, but again, the benefit of the doubt that his friend suffered too many blunt swords to the head, so words did not roll out so smoothly.

"With the stranger, I believe, yeah."

"So you let this man take our friend?" Tillu shook his head wiping the sweat off his brow, "Fucking empty skulled you are," he looked back to his friend, hoping he'd explain more skipping to it.

"All I remember from the traveler, who some how knew me!" He took a swig of the golden canteen, "He said somethin' bout, *Ay! Bald man, I be takin' your friend, you should run,* err somethin' like that."

"He give you that?" Said Tilly eyeing down the canteen wrapped in leather, pierced of gold, and runes that dimly shined, "What's with those runes?"

Edvar looked quickly, glancing the runes, "Oh yeah, forgot bout them," he turned his head curiously looking at them, "I dunno."

"He got you drunk, so he could take Fjorn," Tillu softly said, shaking his head even more, "Gods be damned, Edvar," he let a smile slip his stern face. He knew his friend if offered a free drink, would let anyone talk their way into his head.

"Not anything like that," Edvar said while pushing his stout stomach forward, stretching his back, "Much more to it," he sighed in relief, "Been needing that little crack," he took another sip of the mead.

Tillu was impatient at the point of exhaustion. He knew their was some meaning to the message Edvar was trying to convey. He picked himself up from the chair, walked right over to the fire that burned. He thought of their friend's house that still burned right across the small ravine.

He imagined how heart broken Fjorn would be if he could see what the Jarl had done. *If he could see.*

He looked to his bald friend who still was going at the strange mead. If they left tonight, they'd be clear of the Jarl and his guards, his army, but they had to pack well. They haven't been across the island's gates in some time.

The two friends began walking to the stables in hopes of not drawing too much attention. They needed a couple horses to get out of the village, and maybe into the next, which was a smaller distance north from them.

It was still of the Jarl's domain, his territory, but the Jarl was more focused on Tor at the moment. The North village was known as Boulder's End; the large boulders that held high into the sky, waves from the seas crashing into them. A seaport, which held most of the incoming wealth across Steinsgaard's vast sea. The trading of fish for lumber from the far north was crucial for the Jarl's expanding lands. They hoped to cross the sea into more foreign territory.

Tillu threw up his hood, following Edvar as they approached the stalls full of large brown steeds; tall, full of meat on the legs. They were good for a quick escape. They had endurance, which is why the Jarl used them well. Each had saddles and bags that hung from them.

They picked up their own bags and saddled themselves unto the bulky mares quietly, tying their provisions to the straps for extra capacity. Used for long trips back and forth through the trails.

They quietly kicked their steeds forward slowly striding into the dark forest's trails. They did not look back, just rode fast into the dark dense fog that slung itself into the tall trees.

It was quiet, only the brushing of the winds on trees and bushes sung, along with the hooves silently pounding the dirt road. They both kept to themselves, eyes straight on the road north.

They thought of the Jarl, before and after comparing the sanity of him. Ullfr was known to be mad, but not insane. They thought it was due to growing old in age, but he used to be a companion of theirs when they did raid in the old days.

The Jarl, the one they remembered did an honorable thing of usurping the previous one, Reulf the Wise. He stuck a blade into the back of him, digging into his lungs until he collapsed. It was right after Reulf shamed his own brothers, torturing them all, spiking them against a wall. Arrows pierced their throats. All but Ullfr and the others.

Upset, angered by the ongoing tortures because of minor incidents such as that one; a couple loose cattle, some mead that wasn't theirs they drank, and a couple coin they lost, Ullfr had enough and put Reulf to a dishonorable death.

Everyone, the remaining party including Tillu, Edvar, and Fjorn drank happily that night, and some others drank brightly to the days coming that night. They sang songs in cherish about the act.

As time went on, Ullfr held his course of Jarl. One night it all changed when he came back from a raiding trip. He fell asleep, his skin going grey, sulky, and his eyes filled with blue — changing into the one now known as Ullfr the Mad.

No one questioned it. Right after it all happened, The Jarl built a small cottage up the hills across the bridge, right in between Boulder's Edge and Tor where he spent most of his own time to himself. No wife, no children, he kept a secret life after that.

<u>12</u>

His eyes were held by sleep, he opened them one by one to the odd chatter in the background. Trying to convey his whereabouts. He saw small and stout men; bearded from their pudgy nostrils, down to their chests. Looking rather familiar, but he could not believe what he saw. He thought he was caught in a lucid dream, a sudden illusive imagination he conjured himself. He was surrounded by dwarves!

His head wrenching from unknown amnesia, painful strings that pulled his brain, the small men clambering on small stools, his mind took laps trying to put reality back in the center...

Blending in well due to his height, matching the patrons, he noticed he sat in the corners of the large wide building. He smelled unfamiliar tobacco and spirits. He couldn't grow a beard because of his age, but since the dwarves were too drunk to notice him, it helped Ahlifer to try and carefully leave.

Ahlifer carefully scooted himself out of the wooden booth towards more of the darkened room. He was near a mop and bucket, spilled over on the planks that made up the floor.

He set one foot down, creaking the boards. They loosely shifted as he took each step. Lights from an area below glimmered, dusty particles danced above him as he finally then peeled towards the wall.

He held his back to the musty oaken wall. He turned to another area where it was more darkly lit, quickly scuttling his little legs towards it, hiding once more.

One Dwarf noticed something in the shadowed area of the room. He got from his seat agitated by the weird blinking from the basement, shining its way through the creaks of the unfinished floor.

Ahlifer's heart started to race even more when he held himself behind a tall beam, with the loud footsteps of the dwarf coming his way. He knew he wasn't dreaming, or imagining this, so he ran to the booth once more trying to stay anonymously blended in.

The stout dwarf had a tall wooden mug in his hand, forged with an iron rim. He saw the little boy scuttle through the dark like a rat hiding from a cat. It made him more cautious, yet more curious at what this little figure was up to.

The dwarf brazenly sat in front of the boy who kept his head lowered on the opposite side, "You ain't a dwarf," he smiled seeing the long amber hair flow down Ahlifer's forehead over the hand he kept over his face, "What are you doing here?" He took a sip of his ale awaiting for the boy to speak up.

"Where am I?" Ahlifer asked immediately, hand still blocking his face.

"Rhyven's Inn. A lodge. Silly question." Said the dwarf taking another sip of his drink, "How don't you know where you be? Words seem to coming out well for you," the Dwarf turned his head at a slant trying to look under Ahlifer's hand, "You not be drunk. You not having any ales, nor your hand ain't swellin' from the ores," he set his wooden mug down hard. It splashed onto the table, making a small river that trickled into Ahlifer's lap, "What are you?" He asked again as soon as the boy's hand removed itself to sweep the drink off his lap.

"What am I? What do you mean by that?" Asked Ahlifer, puzzled by the Dwarf's question. "A boy, I guess," he looked away anxiously towards the exit, counting each table honed by other strangers he'd have to pass by for his escape.

"No…" The Dwarf played with his beard, stroking it with a studious face, "I'm a Dwarf. You are no dwarf. So what are you?"

Ahlifer swiveled his head back towards him, having no idea how to answer that question. He remained complacent, but bewildered by such a question. He did not know what the Dwarf meant by what he was.

"Dwarf, me. Yes, I am dwarf," the pudgy man chuckled wiping the remainder of the ale off of the table, "Trolls are trolls, aye?" He danced his two fat fingers along the soaked table, imitating a troll's posture; long strides, long legs, and a little wiggle.

"…aye?" Ahlifer didn't know how to respond.

"Then if a troll is a troll. I be a dwarf, and you be a…?" The Dwarf asked again taking another generous drink.

"You're a dwarf. Troll's a troll… I'm a human," he said quietly back, thinking more than he should have about the question. His head was swelled by the Dwarf's sensical rhetorics. They both spoke the same language, but the difference in diction was a magnificent one.

The Dwarf was baffled when he heard the boy say what he was. Dwarves were never seldom associated with humans, nor did they live among one another, they never even seen one another. They were only told in stories, nothing more.

"A human? Those ones from the stories?" He asked setting his mug down once more, now studying this odd creature before him, "What is a human to be exact?" Only archaic drawings, writings, songs described them — but they never explained what a human *was*.

"I don't know how to describe it. How do you describe what a dwarf is?"

The dwarf became a little more confused at what had the little man across him asked. A dwarf? How do you explain something you already are and are so used to being? It never crossed his mind, "Aye, good point. I have no idea on how to explain what I am to you. How do you know that I'm a dwarf anyhow? I never said I was one."

The Dwarf thought he had a few meads too many due to his lack of comprehension towards this little unknown traveler. He kept drinking anyway, which was in the nature of a dwarf.

The nature of a dwarf, he reminded himself once again, a smile peeking through the brush of his braided beard,

"Dwarves like to drink, boy," He belched loudly, "And we craft things. Once and awhile," he added, belching again, holding his lower belly feeling the rumbling of the ale settling below. He patted his stomach with a hearty well done, "We craft lodges, weapons of wood to whip to iron. We the breed for anyone needin' something done," he finished.

Ahlifer lifted his head up, brushing his greasy hair behind his ears, eyeing the big bearded dwarf down with his bright blue eyes. Fascination caught his pupils. To finally meet a creature from the sagas was a true feat.

"So," Ahlifer coughed, clearing his throat, trying to gain the confidence he needed, "A human eats," he tried to figure out how to explain what he was trying to explain with more easier words. He looked over again at the exit, door opening and closing every second, new patron coming in every second.

"Aye, humans! That's what you are?" Started the Dwarf guzzling down the rest of his mead. He patted his big belly feeling the roars and rumbles once again. He smiled to it when it gurgled and ached, "Another ale here soon, says I," He whisked his beard from the froth that clung to it, "Says you?"

"Says I?"

"Aye, says you. Want a free drink or not?" He said more seriously, hiding back his giddiness, "Us Dwarves take drinkin' more serious than a troll takes treasure," He peered up above to the cracked ceilings, water leaking little droplets onto the tables nearby, "I can not word right. So another ale it is says I."

Ahlifer was completely out of his own comfort zone, and so he nodded slightly back at the strange dwarf in appreciation of the gift the stout man offered.

Was he imagining all of this he wondered, or was it the voice he heard earlier that sent him here? *Kill the Gods.* His head shrieked in cold sweat to remembering what it had told him, right before it had vanished.

 He felt hopelessly lost. He's never drank before, but it felt too him like he did — waking up from a blackness and into a foreign land, or world, or wherever he was felt too strange for his usual perceptions.

"Tell me, human. What are you doing in our land?" The Dwarf slid a mug to Ahlifer, it was overflowing with froth, bubbling up with fresh ale.

Ahlifer didn't know how to respond to that question. He knew he couldn't control his imagination at times, and he always had an answer on why, but right now, he couldn't answer that question — he didn't know why he was there, or what brought him there. He couldn't even remember after his event of the fishing dock where he went under to the bottom; he only remembered the voice and the face of himself dying. Now, he could not control his overthinking mind.

He took a huge drink of his ale, "What am I drinking?" His eyes grew wide, shining brightly from the sobriety that left his white.

"Ale. Never had?" The Dwarf shook his head, "Human's don't drink ale?" He followed with a sip of his own.

Ahlifer reached out to touch his dwarf friend on his rough cheek where his beard had started. The dwarf looked at him, backing away slamming down another ale quickly.

The dwarf now considered humans to be the most curious beings he has ever met. Ahlifer was giving the introduction of the two races a wrong display by acting out of touch.

"Aye, why did you touch me?" Asked the dwarf.

"I wanted to see if you are real."

"I am real, boy. All you humans act so funny?"

Ahlifer shook his head while standing up from his seat and took his leave to the door, stumbling. The dwarf looked uneasily cautious to that.

He took another sip from his thick rimmed ale, and followed another to the empty one Ahlifer left behind. It was in the nature of a Dwarves to *Leave No Ale Left Behind*.

He felt stupid for bringing the little child a drink, if the drink was never meant to be drank. He looked at the boy stumble himself outside the large door, with the other patrons looking oddly at him.

"Ay!" Yelled one of them looking back at the Dwarf who remained in the booth, "Was that just a human you accompanied with, Gufnir?"

Everyone looked back at him sitting in the corner, drinking two ales to himself. Bewildered by what they just saw, they all clambered around each other.

"A human in Svartalfheim?" One asked Gufnir who still sat eyeing the door, hoping for the little boy to come back, "That is not good."

Gufnir sat quietly sipping on his ale, patiently letting the questions flow out of one ear, out the other. He was curious himself what brought the little boy there. No humans were meant to come; the rainbow bridge was meant for Aesir, Vanir, and Gods alike.

Gufnir got up from his booth and excused himself to the basement of the little lodge. He walked down the stairs, each one creaking loudly over the other patron's chatter. He shut the door behind him, the hinges barely hanging. He made sure no one followed him.

"Who were you boy?" He asked himself opening up a dresser with scrolls, paintings, and books.

Gufnir opened a dusty, iron binder; it held more arts, poems, songs that hung from the clamps of years old twine.

One picture after another, one song after another, he kept feeding his stubby fingers through them. '

He stopped on a page, musty with dust and dew, crinkling it, unfolding it back to the page it was.

A painting of a child bearing an aura around him, shaking hands with a Dwarf with a crown, jeweled robes, and axe sheathed on his side. His eyes trickled down tears.

"So you do come to me?" He looked at the page thoroughly, eyes trickling tears, lids flittering to the images.

He closed the book, dismissing himself from the dusty room. Lanterns swooping, flickering to every movement from upstairs, he shut the door behind him tightly, hoping no one else would have the idea to go see what he had been down there for.

13

Ahlifer, stumbling from the ale he had, walking, hiding in the shadows away from the high lamp posts that shined the old stone path in the small, quaint city where he had woken up at.

He kept his distance from the locals that were still out at that time of night trying to dissuade himself of the complications he could create.

He saw the little men walk together in an uncoordinated manner showing that they were just farmers and miners, nothing threatening, but he kept his distance. He stopped behind a little tree out of sight to collect his thoughts.

"Where am I?" He asked himself in attempts to a response from the voice. "Are you there?"

A couple seconds had passed, receiving no word from the voice. He sighed, deeply and frustratingly. He had no idea on where to go, where to hide, how to get home.

He had to find some sort of answer, and it sure wasn't at the inn, for that's what he thought. He looked around the little city made of stone trying to find some sort of explanation of where he was. He didn't see anything due to the darkness that laid upon the night, so he continued to follow the path while remaining out of the light.

He was only still dressed in his lavender tunic he had on, the same he had been wearing when he fell into the water. He needed more to conceal his face though, his hands would not do, and he needed to fully see.

Two dwarves were walking on the stony path a little ways from Ahlifer. They didn't notice the little boy to the side of them, he was in the dark, hiding like a frightened rabbit, concealing itself in the brush.

One of the dwarves wore a long brown coat which went down to his feet. Ahlifer was fascinated by the long coat. Most of his own people never wore those in his small village, nor has he seen any type of clothing like that. The apparel these dwarves wore were to survive the harsh cold mountains, protecting them from the trenches of the mines.

As the two dwarves came to a halt dismissing themselves into separate ways, Ahlifer saw it was a good time to go out of the shadowy streets and make a run for it into the deep woods on the edges.

 In the woods, he'd make a small camp once he made it farther from the unfamiliar civilization. He wasn't much of a survivalist as his sister, Inga was, but he knew the basics of building a fire, a shelter, and so he did just that. He laid quietly on his bed made of leaves watching the fire on his side. He felt the warmth consume him clearing the cold from his blood that the city had given him.

He thought of the Dwarf who he had talked to in the Rhyven's Inn, the same place that he had remembered last since the fall in from the docks. His memories became puzzle pieces, and he was trying to put them together as he watched the fire. He never felt he had to do this, to bring in the reality of such experiences hoping it'd help him find his way home.

He was always so reliant on his imagination to fix things. This time, he had to face reality, and balance his internal emotions, or else, he would never find a way back to his village, or to his family.

He wondered what his father was up to, and Inga, and everyone else; did they know of his disappearance he thought, and were they out looking for him?

He hoped they weren't worrying too much of it. He hated them feeling responsible for his own actions. He remembered Inga always so angered by his imagination and always telling him, "Ahlifer, get your head out your ass, and see what the world has actually given you today!" – He now finally appreciated the angst of those words his sister tried to ingrain into his head. From finding a way out of his mind, now to finding a way out of the world, he had to now use both as allies to survive.

Ahlifer woke up sticky from the warming dew that stuck to him from the early morning sun. He wiped his face with his dirty hands trying to clear it away.
He never remembered a beating sun such as the one he had endured that morning—especially compared to his mornings at his village, this was much hotter. Sticky from sweat and dew, he climbed up from his makeshift bed peering off into the distance of the deep woods to make sure no one was scouting him—he learned this from his Father, "Remember, enemies roam on empty roads."

Dark green trees blanketed the area disallowing a sense of direction of where he was. He was lost.

Hungry, thirsty, and still tired, he knew if he didn't eat, he will be too weak to press on. He looked around bushes that were covered with small red berries hoping he'd not eat a poisonous one—he didn't know what to look for in this unfamiliar land where dwarves dwelled, and humans did not according to the strange dwarf he met.

"Red is good, blue is delicious, green is disgusting", he said to himself over and over. He had had his fair share of poisonous berries that caused vile vomiting and horrid stomach pains, and did not want to repeat that again, and by his experiences, red and blue berries were the good ones, and he hoped it was the same case in this world.

He travelled a little farther into the woods ditching his camp behind him in search of the berries, he was a little farther out from the town he woke up in as well meaning... well, meaning he didn't know where he was or where he was going, but out of sight of people was good.

His tunic was dirty, along with his hands and pants, and his hair was scuffed up making him appear as a hermit who dwelled away from civilization.

Ahlifer was lost in this new world, but thankfully not his mind, as he seemed to feel a lot better due to no more voices from the apparition of himself.

"Old back, old wine, green slacks, how divine!" Sang a rough voice in the trees making Ahlifer crouch immediately, low in stillness spectating his surroundings. He didn't want to be caught for he didn't want to explain anymore of why he was there. His anxiety made him run from such tough conversations.

He hid behind a large curving tree still hearing the voice sing, repeating, and "Old back, and old wine, green slacks, how divine! Old back, old wine, green slacks, how divine!"

Was it a dwarf he wondered? It sounded deeper and gruffer than how the other Dwarves spoke. He kept his distance, but the sound of the forest moving kept coming closer.

"Aye! Who be in my forest? I smell you!" Started the voice in a loud, confirming tone. It didn't sound pleased, and it could smell Ahlifer's presence. He was now concerned and afraid of what this voice belonged to since it could smell him right away, and the more the trees swayed, the voice would ring higher and higher.

"What an odd stench," Said the voice now lowering it's tone, "Something I have not sniffed in awhile," the tree above curved lower, crackling the tiny branches, "Are you a human?" Sniffing again.

It knows the smell of a human? Ahlifer was in complete shock. He only thought that dwarves roamed the lands. He was fully unaware of what home has become. He never was fully awake to know what was going on around him. Naïve and innocent, naturally.

"Human." Laughed the voice in a grumble. "I have not had human for a long time!"

Ahlifer skipped away, falling on his butt, scuttling with two arms away like a grab going back into sea. The tree kept bending, the more he crawled away from whatever kept bending it lower.

He crawled quickly towards the berry bushes, hoping to give the impression that he was just a rabbit startled by sound.

Huge hands came swallowing up his body, gripping his comfortably tight. Two eyes to his, large and blank, he panicked to them; kicking, wriggling and punching.

"A human! How divine!" Said the voice joyously now gripping the boy in its oversized hand. "I have not had a human in a moons age!"

14

Tillu and Edvar stood side by side with their horses tied to trees, sap dripping slowly over the long ropes. They were tired, but this was just the start of the journey. They had to climb down the giant cliff.

They looked down into the void's of the gorge; darkly misty, foggy, and no end in sight.

"Fook me," Edvar bellowed, "Thas' deep."

They were standing on the edge, reflecting the morning sun through their tired eyes. It's been a night or two for them since they escaped the Jarl, they were running on zero sleep.

They could not eat, nor drink— being constantly on the run, they barely even had time to think.

Edvar was craving a bubbly ale, and Tillu was the same, both of their tongues drenched in saliva from thinking about it.

They needed sleep, and more sleep than just a few hours like they have been giving. The ale would have to wait.

"What's down there, ya think?" Asked Edvar with swollen, red tired eyes. He has not been around these edges in ages, since the taking of Boulder's Edge with Ullfr.

"If I'm right, that's where Boulder's End is…" pointed Tillu at small smoke furling from the tall trees that sat underneath them, "We just have to walk down," he sighed to that. His legs could barely move, nor could the horses gallop more steadily without food.

Edvar peeled down again, not afraid of the heights he had to face, "Ah!" He sighed, "Then let's go," he rubbed his swelling eyes now looking to the high, mammoth sized moon that was peaking over some clouds.

They started galloping along the tall cliffs still eyes locked on to the smoke of what could be their sanctuary. Edvar whistled a soft tune, a song from some time ago when things were more peaceful for them. The song was about the God's Protection; a song of Tyr's loyalty to the mortals, and the protection of them through life and death.

He hummed deeply creating a deep tune to the whistling, and they continued to ride further and further around the cliff.

"Tyr, protect us from this gorge. Odin, give me ale," said Edvar tiredly, "Freya, give me women to look at too. Not here on the path, but at that camp down der'," he rambled on, swaying back and forth on his horse, hoping the horse wouldn't keel over from exhaustion.

They had been riding the horses hard, two nights' travels, some stops, but not enough for the horses to regain their strength. They were to determine to make it out of Tor. They were not too fond of being decapitated in the Town Square and held on pikes.

They saw a path with a stoned fence and an old wooden gate with its hinges holding tightly to the doors it held. Edvar got off his horse, starting to whistle again the same song, pushing the gate doors open for them. He pushed hard, trudging the gates beams through the fresh mud.

Tillu started galloping through with Edvar's horse tied to his hand, while his friend held the heavy door open. They both looked down the path seeing it twirl into a spiral, and fog covering it. Edvar looked uneasy to see this so called sanctuary in shambles.

They have not seen Boulder's Edge in quite some time, neither were too sure it even still existed, but being the hard headed pair they were, they pressed on.

"You sure this is it?" Asked Edvar while pulling himself back up on his brown mare. "The place looks in shambles," he saw broken gates, fences, and trees peeling over. The place looking like a graveyard, a recent stage for a battle.

"It has to be," Tillu was not sure if it was a smart idea to press on, but it was their only choice. He always kept a persevering attitude of confidence for his empty headed friend.

"Are you unsure?" Asked Edvar angrily due to his loss of sleep. He thought his friend was not thinking straight from the lack of energy they were running on, "Your eyes tell me you worried, brother," he spat to the side of his mare.

"I'm not unsure, but I'm not sure. This place doesn't seem to be the same since I came here awhile back," Tillu kicked his mare to keep going, slowly but steadily around the the twisting path, "Too many meads since I been here. The last time I seen this place was too many meads as well," he could not get his words out, "I just hope there is a city underneath these trees."

Edvar shook his head in disapproval of this choice. For all they knew, it could be a camp of bandits, hermits, even draugr. They still pressed on picking up the original tune they had been singing, keeping guard as well.

> *Tyr! Mighty warrior of Aesir,*
> *Asgard in ruins,*
> *Yet you hold your balance,*
> *Defense, spear held high.*
> *Actions for actions that are nigh.*

Edvar kept the tune going with harmonious humming while his friend kept the song going, pulling out his long bladed hunting knife sheathed on his leather belt. He looked into his open palm, carving an upwards arrow into the grains of his hand, watching the blood flow slowly out — it was the symbol of Tyr, the Tiwaz, a symbol of protection from the Aesir Tyr. He held the bleeding hand tightly down to his upper pant leg as he travelled farther down the foggy path in search of a city that could be no more.

Hours went by and the sun followed those hours into fading light. They could not see anything besides their horses' heads. They had stopped making their music at this point. They didn't want to attract whatever it was that could be where they were going.

They had their axes, and armor, but two against a camp of bandits would be impossible to survive even with the Tiwaz carved into Edvar's palm. They just kept pressing forward saying prayers in their heads for added protection for the road they travelled hoping no trouble would come.

"It's dark. The sun is still up, but not here. From you're tossed up memory, do you remember if Boulder's End was this dark?" Whispered Edvar over to his friend who barely hung to his horse's strings.

Tillu truthfully didn't know why it was dark and ignored his friend out of spite he would retreat away in regret. He never remembered the journey to the City because of always being liquored up, and he knew he would have remembered going through an eery passage like this one.

"Fuck me, I wish I were drunk now. This ride is going to be the death of me due to the boredom it brings. Does the place have a good mead hall?" Asked Edvar trying to get a reply from his friend.

"Yes. Biggest one you'll ever lie your eyes on," Tillu lied. He personally forgot everything to do with Boulder's Edge. He only remembered the large sea-soaked rocks that guarded the city from the oceans.

Edvar grew a huge smile on his face staring out into the darkness continuing into it. The deeper down the old narrow path, the more darkly it became. The trees were so thick it blocked out the coming afternoon sun. They kept pushing and pushing and pushing though.

Hours went by and so did their mind, gone like the winding roads they left behind. The trail curved and curved, deeper and deeper. Edvar's anticipation for the Mead Hall was what kept him going, and it took the thoughts of discourse away from his mind.

In the beginning, he would have turned back, but the thought of a tasty, bubbly ale around a fire would be quite a treat and reward for his terrible journey. He hoped it were true.

Tillu flopped in his horse with each gallop keeping him awake. He was ready to sleep for months, and eat for years, and drink for centuries. He counted each gallop underneath him as they strolled down the unknowing path.

Fog swept his eyes and his mind. He slapped himself a couple of times to keep himself awake, and to acknowledge he was still alive. In the back of his mind, he had hoped that Boulder's End, another name for Boulder's Edge, was down this path. He regretted the last trip there to be completed blacked out by the mead and ale — he wish he had more of an assertive direction for them.

"What's that, friend?" Asked Tillu slurring his words. He barely hung to his horse, turning with the horse to every twist the path took.

"I didn't say anything," said Edvar looking forward at him who was leaning to the far right of his steed, keeping ahold by turning the leather straps around his left arm. He saw his head raised to the canopies of the trees in an odd trance. "You okay? Want to rest?"

"I be fine."

Edvar kept his eyes on his friend for awhile more unsure of his health — seeing a glowing light towards the bottom of the cliff. He itched his nose trying to open his bloodshot eyes more to see what it could be. It could be a torch he thought, or it could be a wisp. "A wisp?" He said to himself in laughter. "Bloody wisps!" He laughed repeatedly in his head. His mind started to run away from him. As he got closer, Tillu was now on the left side of the horse laughing frantically into the sky, "Odin be good, Freya be good," he took a deep hard breath, "Loki, fuck you if you try to fook' this up for us."

The more they rode down the spiny path, the more torches they saw revealing a camp of some sort, and eventually a giant wall and gate; and unlike the one they saw before, this gate and wall were much more intact. Two guards in high watch towers on each side behind the large wall, and two guards on the outside on each side of the gate looked at the two men on horse cautiously; Tillu barely on his horse laughing to himself, and Edvar staring up to the sky.

"Aye! You horse riders!" Started the guard on the right of the gate who was dressed in a long blue cloak wearing a wolf pelted garb, padded down with metal armored shoulders. "What in the bloody hell are you two doing over there?" He shifted his full attention of his squad to them, "Fuckin' draugr be out there!" They kept their defense, arrows latched onto their bows, spears held out.

The two kept galloping oblivious to the guardsmen talking to them; riding slowly coming out of the fog in sight, stopping in front of the two guards. The horses neighed tirelessly from the miles of riding they had done. Tillu fell off his horse onto the muddy ground, rolling to his back, falling right to sleep.

"Trying to find passage to Boulder's End," laughed Tillu face smothered in mud while Edvar finally fell asleep on his horse.

"Skin is still white, no pale! No blue in their eyes!" Yelled the guard observing the two men who fell asleep.

"Let them in?" Asked the guard next to the portcullis that held high by a chain.

"Aye! They just drunken by sleep. Bring them to the Jarl!" Said the guard again, "Bring their horses to the stables as well!"

"They ridin' from Tor. Must be poor folks trying to see what they can do about it," the guard sheathed his bow, unlatching the arrow first.

The guards signaled for the gate to open immediately bringing in the two weak men along with them. They put Tillu up on one of their shoulders, and guided his horse with him, while Edvar sleeping was rode in on his. It wasn't Boulder's End they landed in, but a small militaristic-like camp. Unaware of everything going on, they slept it off that entire night and into the next late afternoon awaking in a tent full of axes and maps.

Edvar sipped on some warm mead awakening his common senses—while Tillu ate spit fired boar that was left over from the previous night from the guards' dinner. They didn't talk much among each other, they were too focused on regaining their strength, by eating a lot of boar and drinking a lot of mead.

They knew the Jarl was going to be searching Boulder's End next, and they knew he wouldn't stop there until they were answered for, not unless he found Fjorn first which added more of a trivial struggle to their journey.

One tall, and lanky bearded man came into the tent where they were recouping their hunger and thirst. He was a burly man with a long blue cloak just like the guards at the gate, but his had a symbol of an eagle on it.

He was much more important due to the fact his cape had a special sigil—the two were unfamiliar with it, but they kept their hungry eyes on it while they slurped their meads, and swallowed their haunches.

They nodded to him, welcoming his presence. What any low folk would do to a higher up.
They had no idea who he was, but they showed a brotherly respect to all men who dawned the beard and axe—and authoritative sigil.

"Riding down The Witch's Spine?" Started the man dressed in the blue cloak. He sat down at their tiny table, grabbing an ale for himself.

"Aye, if that's what that fucking path was called, then, aye, yes," said Edvar still unsure who this stranger was and nerved from the trek.

"Travelers?" Asked the man.

"Yes," said Tillu.

"Where are you from?"

"Thor's Heart," replied Tillu, "Tor, whatever you Northerners call it." He kept his confidence, yet remained with his resolve of honor.

The man scratched his head in a curiosity, showing he was unfamiliar with what Thor's Heart was, or even Tor.

He poured himself water on the side, casually bringing his chair closer to the conversation. He took a big drink of the water, then followed it with ale.

"You survived a passage into this region that none other survive," he said. "You two looked like you fucked the witch who this here passage was named after," he laughed, "That passage takes a week to traverse, and that's going down, which you two did," He paused looking at the two hungry men, "The thing is, how in the Gods' name did you survive without rations and provisions?"

"I have an axe, a knife," Edvar said brightly as if the man would dismiss them right there, or dismiss himself. Edvar hated conversation when his belly was empty.

The man whose prominence shined through was bewildered by the two's trek. The path they rode on wasn't meant for any mortal to withstand without the right equipment, and the reason for the ridge's name wasn't to be taken lightly.

The man served them some mead from a wooden jug expecting some truth out of them. He didn't know why they were there, and by taking immediate concerned pointed him as the Leader of the small camp. He set his axe to his side, on another chair showing a sign of acceptance, trust, and honor — a formidable gesture.

"We just be needin' to get to Boulder's Edge," said Edvar. "And my dear friend, Tillu here said this be the correct route."

"You speak too much, Edvar," Tillu whispered back remembering when he let Fjorn go for a cool drink of mead.

The man shuddered and quickly went for his cup of mead taking a huge gulp of it. Something was on his mind that disturbed him with those words of "Boulder's Edge".

"Haven't heard that name in quite some time," he said back.

"What do you mean? Are we not in the right course?" Asked Tillu with no hesitation due to the self-embarrassment creeping on. He thought this was the way, the path of twists and turns always was the course led to The City.

"Boulder's Edge fell months back to me," responded the man. "The name's Krevii. I'm the Jarl of what used to be Boulder's Edge," he smiled to the uneducated men, "Tor though, that's mine as well, that was a couple weeks ago, it claimed as mine." He smiled wiping the froth off his intricately trimmed mustache.

The two friends looked at each other with complete unawareness of their situation and what the strange man meant by those words.

They thought it was still occupied by Ullfr. They felt smaller than they already were; poor, uneducated folk from the villages south.

"I thought it belonged to Ullfr the Mad?" Questioned Tillu. He was confused more, setting his drink and food down, sliding them away from him. He wanted to remember these words this man speaks.

"No, not anymore since I killed him myself with my hands about a week or two ago when I claimed Tor," proudly Krevii flashing his axe near his side. "This axe remains what is left of The Mad Jarl." The axe was Ullfr's, branded with his families crest of runic symbols.

Edvar and Tillu's head spun from the mead, in dismay that was brought unto them by Krevii's words. The Jarl was dead? For how long? How long have they rode from the escape of Ullfr? With everything going on, the time they spent on the road, the lack of sleep had set them off.

"How do you know it were Ullfr? We come from Thor's Heart in retreat from him!" Said Tillu.
"I have his axe right here. My knife that still has his blood in what was called Boulder's City, now turned into Ullfr's Rest," said Krevii still in illusion of what his two visitors had experienced. "What do you mean you are running from him?"

"Fook man, did you burn his body?" Edvar stated going back to ripping apart the boar he was filling his belly with.

The Jarl, Krevii looked embarrassed. He did not think of it, he was hoping it would have been a mark of power to keep the dead Ullfr's body at the spot he was slained. He ignored that question.

"Two day ride. That's the tops we endured. Two fucking days. On the first, we said our goodbyes to the Mad Jarl and then stole his horses and now we are here. He's trying to hunt our brother!" Said Tillu frantically concerned for his own words.

Krevii looked dumbfounded, "Thor's Heart is a Free Man's world… I don't have anything to do with that since I took care of Ullfr." He picked up his axe and smacked it against his shoulder while he sat and sipped his mug of mead, "That man became mad. More than before he was given the title. I did what was right," he sighed wiping his hair back, feeling perplexity creep up on him.

He saw the two going mad themselves before him, and he felt a little sorry for them. He didn't know what else to say to calm their minds.

Edvar got up from his chair, looking out of the tent in paranoia. Darkness, trees, fog dancing all together to the sun that peeled through.

He didn't feel good about the situation they were in. He has never even heard of the name Krevii, but, if it were true that Ullfr was dead… then they would have ever got news of a new Jarl unless if he visited them on the island of Thor's Heart. Panic had set in, and it was a constant panic that they were in more trouble than they were.

"Can you take us to whatever the fuck you call it now?" Asked Edvar in a nervous yet frustrating voice. He wanted to see what the place looked like, and still was counting on a great mead hall to feast and drink at.
He didn't know what else to say after that. He couldn't trust this man Krevii just yet. Or was it his mind that he couldn't trust? He stopped thinking.

"Aye, tomorrow morning," replied Krevii acting absurdly suspicious, "We have a caravan that comes in from this camp to the port."

They had to humor him a little more and make their way off by themselves. Steal a couple horses first, while the sneaky bastard was sleeping and head off later that night. It would be hard they knew that, but they knew that Krevii was just playing dumb.

Once the Jarl left their tent, that afternoon, they couldn't hold back from saying what was on their minds, "Fucker, be hiding something from us!" – they said it at the same time staring eye to eye from each of their cots, sitting in a slumped position, heads hanging low.

"You speak too much," Tillu patted his friend's back hoping that'd give him a good lesson, "You and your damned mead."

"It wasn't the damned mead, it's more of what is going on is what killing my sobriety."

They were too far paranoid from every stranger they met, and even the ones they knew, or thought they did, on account that Ullfr may be dead, and that was a ghost who was chasing them. They needed a drink, but they couldn't, last thing they wanted was to be drunk off their asses while escaping.

They had no idea where to go now. Boulder's Edge was not a thing anymore, or could they trust that word from Krevii since they had little trust in him in the first place. All they knew was that they had to go. Maybe back to Thor's Heart thought Edvar convinced they could then displace the thoughts that the Jarl was actually dead, and time was just not on their side.

Tillu objected that notion instantly, and decided for them to make their way east, towards the ocean and some how sail to Northern Steinsgaard, Vosno the Capital; a large city that was full of wealth, rich folk, and would be a perfect place for two men to hide out in.

Edvar agreed and cursed his mangled skull that he didn't think of that option. To Vosno by boat, and hide from the insanity of the South.

<u>15</u>

Inga stared at the rickety old boat that Odin told her to escape in. She thought it had to be a joke due to one missing oar, and the cracks in the sides of the hull that would burst at any time if she sat in.

She wiped the sweaty mud from her forehead and shook her head. She slowly got in it, first testing it out with her right leg—it seemed fine, then she tried the second, and low and behold it stayed afloat in the shallow creek. The question was now, how would it fair once she got into the ocean? Or was the wind going to take her to the ocean? She was supposed to let the current take her… but to where?

She gently sat down cautiously on the bending benching in the middle of the boat—it seemed fine. Nothing pressed or creaked, and it didn't wobble in a peculiar way. It definitely could take her to the ocean, but again, was it supposed to?

Her first thoughts immediately upon being proved wrong was *Do not question the Gods, damnit! Odin at that, Inga.* She sat in the boat with Ratatoskr now perched on her shoulder, him quickly surveying the boat as if he expected too that it would sink as soon as she got in.

"Guess your at a healthy weight," said Ratatoskr still looking around the boat from her shoulder.

"Shut it."

The two just sat in the boat, bobbing back and forth from the tiny winds. Inga looked around the forest seeing if any other gust would bring them on their journey, but it did not come. She then dipped her hands in the fresh cold water and wiped off the remaining mud on her face. She sighed.

She was angry with herself for leaving to early, and not waiting for a sign from Odin. She started to get up from the boat but an intense gust of wind blew her back down on her bottom, and little Ratatoskr in the front.

He hurled in a somersault motion, and landed cleanly as if it were no big deal. Stubbornly she grabbed the one green oar and started to dig under water and into the rocks trying to push the boat forward, but it did not budge.

"Seriously!" She said.

"I think you gotta wait," replied Ratatoskr while hopping back up on her shoulder   .

"I don't even know what to wait for!"

Ratatoskr could sense the urgency in her voice so he knew not to say anymore in fear he'd piss her off much more.

She was stubborn indeed and it made things worse for herself at this time. She needed to wait for a sign from Odin, she knew that much, but what was the sign she'd receive? It had to do with nature… A talking squirrel was a likely sign, but he was there coincidentally.

Ratatoskr was just hungry and paid no mind in the God's plan, unless it had to do with food or gossip, he'd be in. But, the things he could tell his buddies about how the God's were using mortals for their plans to capture Loki would have been a divine chat, but he felt for the girl, and he felt as if he needed to help her forward.

The nature seemed as if it wanted them to sit it out in the merely tarnished row boat, and Inga wasn't having that. She felt as if she was in a time-out by the nature itself, for every time she tried to leave the boat, a wind blew her back down to her seat.

She threw the oar into the water in arrogance towards the situation.

She felt panicked, and out of touch with her own reality from the anxious outbursts.

She wanted to go wherever Odin was sending her, even if she had not the slightest idea where it would be, her adventurous heart pounded to the thought of a new journey.

Deep down her, she would miss her father, especially not knowing of his own safety and that he had been carried off by Odin himself, for he did not explain that part of the plan. She was more focused on her older brother, Ahlifer at this point.

She knew Tillu and Edvar would take care of her father, and she also didn't even know about their whereabouts as well. She felt as if this plan was for the safety of all of them, but little did she know, it was not about the mortals, but the Gods.

The forest began to tremor, leaves blowing east, and birds singing in an odd manner. She felt the cold water spit up on the sides from the winds gliding on the creek. If this wasn't the "sign" for them to leave, then what would it be. The boat steadily creaked forward sounding as if it would sink right there. Inga held tight on the sides of the boat as her and Ratatoskr were gently pushed down the little river.

It was the sign she thought, and the adventure was about to begin! She was nervous, yet relieved she was on her way, and happy she can now help Ahlifer... hopefully — Odin never mentioned if she would see her brother again. She knew wherever she was going, it would be safer for her to find him from there.

The boat cracked and growled as the speed picked up. Inga grabbed the green oar in her left hand as she watched herself sail down the forest. She felt the winds change into a new direction hitting her from the west, and was stunned by how she wasn't flipped from one side. It must have been some sort of magic at play, she thought.

Ratatoskr didn't like the winds one bit, and flipped himself down to the front of the boat, hiding from the rapid gusts. If it were magic, it only worked to protect Inga, and not the little squirrel.

"Where we going?" Asked Ratatoskr still unaware of what he agreed to.

"I have not the slightest," replied Inga holding steadily as the boat ride became fiercer.

Ratatoskr felt the boat churn, and whip from the winds. He looked up at Inga's face of uncertainty.

He then regretted this adventure; probably should have completed searching for nuts, finding out some mortal gossip, and continued to stay out of these endeavors that were now inevitable to back out of. There was no more time for chat for the bumpy ride made it hard to.

He watched Inga bounce back and forth hitting the aura's surrounding the boat, and only he could sense them due to him being closer to the God's blood line — he wasn't related to them by any means, but he came from the world tree just as they did.

Inga was thrown to the front smashing her head on the hull, but she did not feel pain because of the magical barriers that protected her from so. She was now finally optimistic as she took the blow to her head; she didn't feel anything from it, and was surprised from it — she knew that the adventure, the journey, her destiny was coming to play. Not every mortal was lucky enough to get a calling from the God's and she prided that, and most of all feeling invincible during the journey due to the magic protection around her. She thanked Odin under her breath as she got up from being smacked real hard.

Ratatoskr gasped aloud as he saw the mortal get up from being flown into the front and getting back up without a mark. He was perplexed by the way she took the hit to her head even though he knew the magic protected her from getting knocked out. It was actually funny to him afterwards — he had a cynical humor especially involving someone in pain. He felt bad for them, but it always brought laughter to his eyes when he saw someone clumsily getting hurt.

"That was pretty funny!" Said Ratatoskr trying to drown out the gusts of winds alongside him.

Inga just smiled at him ignoring what he meant from it and kept her eyes straight ahead on the… waterfall coming up, "Waterfall!" She screamed at the top of her throat.

They hurled down the waterfall bouncing back and forth across the auras. Ratatoskr was lucky enough to claw into Inga's tunic bracing himself so he didn't fall off for he was immune to the magical barriers.

Inga laughed aloud as they made a clear landing with the rickety old boat still intact after their huge fall off the falls. She didn't expect to be alive after that bit, but she was happy they were.

They now were gently floating in the middle of an enormous strange body of water. Inga brushed her hair back and looked around — it were an ocean they landed in, and the waterfall was in no clear sight. If only Ahlifer would have been able to take part in her adventure, she wished to herself. She didn't know where he was, nor if he was safe, but knew he would soon be once could she find out how to get to him.

"Gods' where are we?" Asked Inga crawling around the small boat trying to spot some sort of land they could build camp at. She had no recollection or memory of where they were; from the small creeks in her woods, to unfamiliar ocean.

"Oh boy," said Ratatoskr.

"What?"

"I know where we are. Notice that no birds fly here?"

Inga looked around trying to find a single bird in the sky. Most birds flew peacefully over the sea awaiting fish for their dinners. She also noticed the sun was bigger and brighter.

"Where are we?" Inga finally replied.

"Coast of Jotunheim."

"The Giants world!?" She said in a nervous tone of excitement. She never expected to end up in a place like that. She tried to hold back more of her excitement.

Ratatoskr just nodded looking north of them at the big ball of fire that shined so brightly, but not brightly enough to warm the cold chills that shuddered through their skin.

Due to the wide oceans of Jotunheim to Asgard, the air was thinned out by a cold sheet of ice, and a wall of naturally carved mountains. Where they were, they did not see any of those, but ocean. They were far out, and they had to figure out where to go now.

Odin never gave Inga concise information of where to go besides of getting in the little row boat and letting the currents take her to the place she needed. Jotunheim though? She wondered, why Jotunheim? That is the enemy of the Gods, and an enemy of the mortals by birth.

She had to further question her actions on the course she was taking, and to make sure the path she was taking was the right one.

They floated gently in the boat with nothing in sight. No birds, no sounds, just the cracking of the old boat teetering back and forth to the icy currents. They had no map, no idea on where to go, so they sat with the one oar that sat on Inga's lap.

One oar wasn't going to get them anywhere, and they had no idea where it could have been, or even if it existed. They sat for hours and hours in the cold, frosty airs lost out in the middle of an unknown sea.

Ratatoskr perched back up on Inga's shoulder with an acorn he saved for his travels, nibbling at it, and chewing the shell, savoring the flavors of it all.

"How do you know this is Jotunheim's coast?" Asked Inga. "Have you even ever been?" She was puzzled with her little companion's ambiguous knowledge.

"Never been. Just heard about it from the eagle."

"Eagle?"

"Yes, the eagle who sits on the top of the world tree. We are friends, or so I think we are. He doesn't seem to like me until I tell him shit the dragon tells me."

"The dragon? I thought dragons were myths?" She asked trying to fathom it all. It was all beyond her own measure of thinking.

"Myths? What are myths? No, dragons are real — and so are giants, and trolls, and the like."

Inga felt out of touch with reality for all the sagas she knew were coming to life. First meeting a god, now a talking squirrel who schmoozes with a dragon and a giant eagle, and now to giants.

Seeing was believing though for her, and she needed to see the giants herself, to help her curiosity and to quell her questioning conscience. It wasn't natural to assume things were true until she saw them first hand — unlike her brother who assumed every story was true, and living.

"So, if we are close to Jotunheim, we are close to Asgard?" Asked Inga.

"Yes," said the squirrel still chewing on the shell of his acorn. "Pretty close, but if you

want to make it from sea to Asgard, then you're in for a trek."
　　　　　　　　　　　　　　　"How so? Can't we just go the opposite way of Jotunheim?"
　　　　　　　　　　　　　"No, the Gods aren't that stupid to leave the waters open for their enemies. They have a huge wall surrounding them, and not to mention the magical shit they have hovering around it. If you want to reach the Gods, we have to go through the land of the giants."

　　　Inga wasn't pleased by that, but she did want to meet a giant. Not all giants were angry drunkards according to the sagas, but most of them just wanted to live peacefully in their small villages, just as mortals did.

　　　They had a little more freedom though, they weren't under the Gods control, nor were they ever going to be.

　　　Mortals were in a sense — they felt as if they should be considering the Gods gave them life. The sagas also talked about the humans' role in Ragnarok; which was the end of times, the final battle where everything is put to rest, and new races are born.

　　　The two still floated in the cold oceans of Jotunheim with Inga contemplating on what to do from there, and Ratatoskr just chewing away on his acorn. If they landed on the wrong shores, they could be in trouble because some of the shores in Jotunheim are where most giants live.

　　　If they don't go to a shore, they would die out in sea. Inga had to make up her mind, and soon because once the large sun had settled, they would no doubt freeze to death. Inga had no supplies, nor provisions to survive out in the ocean as well… which made her row the boat with one oar in haste towards the north-east of the ocean.

　　　"So we are going to giant land?" Asked Ratatoskr seeing her stubbornly paddle with the one oar.

　　　"Yes, for if we don't, we will starve. I'll probably end up eating you, and I consider you as a friend, so I'd rather not do that," she replied with a cynical smile.

　　　"Well, shit. Paddle! Paddle! — I wouldn't have come with you if your plan was to eat me this whole time. Come to think of it, it does make sense now. I bet I taste like acorns and shit — because I need to shit. To defecate. I've been holding it in this whole entire ride.

How long do you think we've been out here? It feels like ages. Maybe I'll poop on some old giants' forehead once we make it to shore. That'd be pretty funny. *Little fookin' squirrel shat on me head!* I'm sure he would say."

"Stop talking for awhile. Come up with a plan to piss of a giant when we make land. Don't include me in it though. I'm here to find the Gods, and not to die from a nasty Giant with shit on its head."

Ratatoskr laughed to himself in a high pitched tone and giggled to the fact that he finally was able to go back to his old self of pissing people off. He loved it, and he felt as if that's what the Gods wanted of him, but now he thought—maybe there is more to his life, maybe he was supposed to guide this girl to the Gods.

He felt incredible, and proud of himself; happy to be apart of a new tale someone could write, a new song, a new saga. A new saga that has not been foretold, sang, or spoken... and it included the fouled-mouth, gossiping squirrel, Ratatoskr.

Inga's arms were already getting weak and the two barely made a significant distance from when they fell from the mysterious waterfall. Inga just set in the oar on her lap in anger, she knew they weren't making progress. One oar wouldn't do. They needed something else to help guide them.

Those magical winds sure would have helped at that moment, but they were no longer; it was just cold breezes, and thick sun that shined on them, and it didn't help their course one bit. Inga looked around the empty boat for something to press on. She saw a hole with water that didn't flow through it.

"Waters not coming through."

"Yes. We are not in the water. We are in a boat," said Ratatoskr sarcastically.

"No, look at this hole. If this were a normal boat, the water would have seeped through now," she said pointing out the medium sized hole under her seat. The magical aura must have been still present. Was this boat actually supposed to guide them to where they were, or was it the barrier? She thought. She was now aware how the boat actually stayed afloat.

She started tearing the sides of the boat apart,

cracking the old oak into a long board which would serve as the second oar. Ratatoskr laughed to the fact she was tearing their ride apart, he knew Odin wasn't going to just let them die.

He cursed himself for not thinking more of it, until she acted. Inga held the board up high blocking the sun examining it. The suns rays turned glowing around it, transforming it into another oar. It was green... the missing oar. Inga was dumbfounded by the magic, but she didn't dwell on it, and instead started paddling east, towards the shores of Jotunheim.

<u>16</u>

"What do we do with him?" Asked Tyr as he watched Odin lay down the dying man on a long wooden altar. He looked into his eyes; burning white, sightless, and blind.

Fjorn was dying by the cursed glow around his body that only the Gods could sense and that is why Odin brought him there, to study him, and to see if this would lead to Loki's whereabouts.

"His eyes see something different than what we see, and we need to see through those eyes. It may point us towards Loki, or it may not," said Odin while starting to cut Fjorn's shirt with his hunting knife.

The knife shined with runes so it could not pierce the flesh in case of an accidental slip. He threw the torn up shirt to the side revealing Fjorn's chest full of red glowing runic marks.

They were burned to his chest, and not from metal, but from magic — magic that only came from Muspelheim, the domain of the fire giant, Surtr.
"That magic…" said Tyr cautiously. "Why is it on him? Has Loki made a pact with the fire giant himself, do you think?"

"We do not know until we know, Tyr. Do not assume the worse, but assume the worse." Odin always sounded as if he talked in code with his brethren. It were only the knowledge and wisdom coursing in his veins that made him speak so, especially when such rhetorics were given.

Tyr just nodded in agreement, hand clutched to his sword. Odin continued examining Fjorn's unmoving body, carefully cutting off his trousers — nothing was there out of the ordinary, and that was good.

If it was Surtr, it meant terrible tidings were to come, for they have never been in contact with the fire giant since the beginning of time, and the prophecy was, the next time they saw him was on Ragnarok — Loki was that clever to bring him in. For selfishly wriggling his way out of the hands of justice and including the death bringer himself.

Odin trembled at the thoughts of death among the

Aesir, Vanir, and the world. It was too soon he thought, but, Loki would do anything to sly out of consequences; and if that meant bringing the world to the end to escape his own punishment, he would. Odin carefully felt out the burning runes on Fjorn's chest feeling the auras emit a cold wave.

He didn't understand why they branded the man's chest and blind him to never see the world as was again, and instead see a world full of terror as it was supposed to be. Once he would awake, he would be in a terrible pain; from the sight of the dead walking to the eternal pain of those runes branded into his chest.

Odin nor Tyr knew what the runes did to him, but they knew the magic instilled into them would cause internal torment; physically, and emotionally. Tyr felt bad for the mortal, but he did not say it, and he has never felt for another until now.

Odin did as well, and would say it, but he had no time to mention his sympathy towards the dying man. Asleep, and slowly tortured by those runes burned to him, killing him.

Did he feel anything emotionally or physically? The Gods never saw anything like this before, so they had no way of telling.

"Loki did this. This is magic from Muspell, and runes of Loki. I'm certain of it. Whatever Loki's plan is, it's Ragnarok. Our deaths are soon, Tyr," said Odin with a long saddened face. "We need to find the traitor before this can occur, and we will torture him until we declare Ragnarok ourselves! I will not allow him to pick and choose anymore!" Odin fell into a rage, set on from his worrying mind.

Tyr knew nothing good was going to happen from the sign and sight of the man that laid before them. But why did he go and do this to a mortal was the real question. Why bring in Midgardians thought Tyr when he could have done this differently. In the end, they knew that Loki knew what he was doing.
"Even your wisdom can't fathom the ideas of The Son of Laufey," said Tyr.

"Unfortunately too or else I would have had him dead centuries back," laughed Odin.

The two smiled with uncertainty of what the future was going to bring. First, they needed to get Fjorn back to the living seeing if he had answers for them.

Panicked in pain he'd awake seeing the lights of the dead, and the voices; he'd be startled at first, and confused, and irritated, but they had to.

Odin walked down the great halls of Asgard to the Rainbow Bridge where Heimdall stood keenly at his post where he would guard Asgard from the giants. He had an emotionless face upon him with horns high mounting upon his bronzed helmet, and a staff large as an average sea serpent.

Odin greeted him. He knew Heimdall would know of the future for he could see the whole world where he stood, and knew what went on.

"My friend, any signs of the betrayer?" Asked Odin referring to Loki.

"No, but the mortal girl is on the coasts of Jotunheim as we speak."

"Finally some good news, even if it isn't the spotting of Loki. Is she close to the cave?"

"Close, but she will not make it by the sun's end," replied Heimdall still fixed towards the long bridge of many illuminating colors.

"I will fix that, but right now, do you know what will come to us by the end of the week?" Said Odin in a nervous curious voice. If anyone would know anything, it'd be Heimdall at this moment for he sees everything of the nine worlds.

"I can not tell you that my friend. We can not reshape our future as Aesir's. Just like mortals we also serve a purpose, and that is to serve this universe, and the nature of it."

"We think Loki is bringing the end of our times closer than we think, but those are just assumptions, and you know as well as I do, I hate assuming what the future will bring."

Heimdall patiently stood tall looking out towards the lands below him of Asgard, to Midghard, to the realms of Hel; he had seen it all, and kept all the secrets to himself.

He knew of what was coming, but he did not want to share with the other Aesir for fear that their stubbornness and pride would change the tides of their destinies. It was the little he could do for them.

Odin understood, so he excused himself from Heimdall's presence and returned to Tyr and the body of Fjorn.

Tyr was examining Fjorn's body closer when Odin walked in. He bore his sword in his one hand in case of foul play, or that the body was a draugr: a dead being who still walks.

Odin unapologetically moved Tyr out of the way so he could look closer at the lifeless body holding his hunting knife made of gold steel, and began carving into his forehead a *Ansuz* symbol — a symbol of the Aesir. He wanted to see if it emitted the same energy the other scars did, but it did not.

He then waved Odin for Tyr to carve a *Tiwaz* into his forehead next to the *Ansuz*. For protection from the God's he declared as Tyr finished the final stroke with the knife. Fjorn's head covered now in blood trembled and shook, his eyes projecting bright lights.

"Where am I?" Awoke Fjorn eyes fully bright.

Odin had no choice to do what he did, and it were the last resort. He didn't know if it was going to alter the magical properties in Fjorn's body or not, but he had to get answers.

Even though Fjorn spoke, it did not mean he was alive, or was going to make it. He was in another realm of the dead.

"Where are you?" Asked Odin seeing his soul walk through the bones of Hel.

"I don't know."

Tyr held his sword even tighter, gripping it in fear. He was always ready for the unexpected.

"What do you see?" Asked Odin again.

"I see… I see the dead, and living walking amongst one another," He took a huge worried breath in, "Why? Why do I see this?"

"Do you remember what happened?"

"No," said Fjorn lying still on his back eyes aglow haunted by his visions, "I do not."

"What was your last memory?" Asked Odin once again. He felt as if he was getting closer to what was going on with the man. He had to keep pressing for more truth.

Fjorn's mouth did not move while he talked. It was his soul that pulsed the vocal chords from his throat into the energy of the world. He neither did move, nor show any sign of life.

"My memory? I do not have one. I just remember this place. Scarred, tormented, my body aches to be let go, and it needs to begone. The future I see, and if you call memory, that is my future."

Odin and Tyr perplexed by Fjorn's answers wondered now if it were really Fjorn talking. They only wanted to find out where their fellow Aesir has gone to and what his motives were, and why he brought the mortals of Midgard into it. Fjorn just like Odin, would not give clear answers which made it tough for them to figure everything out.

"Your memory serves as your future?" Asked Odin and then thought to himself, "The man's memory serves for his future? Can he see what is to come? Is this some sort of warning?"

"I see the future, a song of it, I don't know the words, but I can hear them, but for some reason I can not repeat them. It burns the touch of the tongue, and aches the body, but rejoices the ones who won," said Fjorn still eyes glowing bright and body paralyzed by the magic.

Tyr and Odin looked wide eyed at each other as if it were true, the end of times, Ragnarok. They knew Fjorn couldn't see them so they dismissed themselves out of the room to quietly talk amongst each other.

Odin for one didn't feel right, as if he felt his body begin to slowly deteriorate. It felt like the middle, and not the beginning.

Time was not with them, but maybe they could make it their ally. They could use Fjorn's bountiful wisdom of the future to their advantage, but how they were going to do that was the main question.

"He said, a song. A song of the future? Burns the tongue?" Said Odin contemplating.

"Aches the body. Metaphor perhaps?" Added Tyr.

"Can not hear it, but can..."

"Bragi. He knows of songs. We must get Bragi," said Tyr trying to help get closer to a solution, "I shall go fetch him."

Odin agreed. They needed the God of Song, and Poetry. He also could read the runes of which burned immensely unto Fjorn's chest. They now knew they needed

Fjorn alive, for he could serve as a valuable tool in this scenario, and maybe later a weapon.

Tyr removed himself from Odin's presence, and started his search for Bragi, while Odin remained in the hall that glowed with torches made of dwarven metals. It helped put an ease to his mind watching the glowing, green lighting hover around the room. He finally felt calm.

<u>17</u>

Ahlifer sat up in the tall tree colored in maroon bark. The giant hand had put him up there, and didn't let him down, nor could he get down, he'd fall to his death.

The huge hand belonged to a overgrown man, a troll, with long black beaded hair, and a couple warts to fill its unnatural complexion.

The troll was eating an ox, not alive thank the gods praised Ahlifer to himself as he watched the huge troll eat furiously, leaving bits and pieces of the carcass below.

"Am I next?" Asked Ahlifer hesitantly.

The troll stopped chewing, took a huge gulp out of a giant hand-crafted mug full of mead and shook his head politely at the little boy in the tree. He then went back to eating the haunches of the remaining ox.

Ahlifer looked very confused. Why did this troll grab him, setting up on the tallest branch of the tree? Was it just to watch him eat? – He has never seen a troll in his life, nor did he expect to. He thought they were just in the stories, the days of the old, but clearly to his surprise they were not.

The troll finished his ox throwing the rest of the carcass on the ground, and took another huge gulp of his mead in relief that he was filled. He wiped his grimy mouth, clearing the blood and guts that spilled from his lips.

He smiled at the boy and grabbed him, bringing him to another branch of another tree. Ahlifer was nervous that he was just going to become bait, or food, or just a toy to this troll, he had no idea of the nature of trolls.

"What are you doing out here?" Asked Ahlifer trying to get an idea of what the troll's intentions were.

"I'm eating."

"I see that."

"Should I not feast when I finally get to see a human again?" Asked the troll politely.

The troll was oddly mild-mannered, and gracious towards Ahlifer, and that is what caught little Ahlifer off guard. The troll just wanted to eat with company; a human at that, and apparently he's done it before some time ago. Ahlifer came to realization that the troll was lonely.

"So, when you said never had human in awhile?

You meant…" Ahlifer was confused whether that human was meant for dinner, or simply just a traveling guest.

"Haven't had one as a guest in some while. Don't listen to those nasty Dwarves what they say bouts us trolls. Not all of us want to suck the blood dry from living beings."

"The ox…" added Ahlifer.

"The ox is all I eat. Too many of them to count in these damned surrounding fields."

Ahlifer watched him pick up another ox, slipping the dead animal into his long curving mouth. The troll licked its' fingers in pleasure, and took a sip of his mead to wash it down.

Ahlifer was hungry, but he didn't want to eat uncooked ox, and even so ask the troll for dinner; he hadn't known the customs of the troll species, or how to properly act accordingly around one, so he just watched the troll eat.

The troll snapped a branch off of a tree next to him, and used it to pick clean his teeth from the fur of the ox, and guts. Ahlifer shuddered to the sight of it, he smelled the stench of day old ox meat and blood, and of whatever else the troll fancied that day.

The day was getting longer, and Ahlifer was getting hungrier. He needed to eat something soon or else he would be too weak to continue his travels to wherever he was going. The troll maybe knew more of the lands, but

Ahlifer didn't want to ask him in fear of this strange creature's mood; the troll was nice, and pleasant, but coming from the stories, their moods could swing at any given moment.

Instead, Ahlifer just sat on the tree branch watching the troll do his "troll things" — from eating every 20 minutes a fresh ox, to drinking gallons of mead, and sometimes talking to Ahlifer.

"So, human. How did you get here to these lands?" Asked the troll licking its fingers dry.

"I don't know. I awoke in a tavern full of dwarves."

"Sounds to me you never seen a dwarf before."

"Neither a troll like you."

The troll grabbed little Ahlifer off the branch and started walking, earth trembling towards a cliff overlooking a lake which shined of beauty as if the water were crystals itself.

Ahlifer had never seen a lake like that in his life, and was in awe of it. He felt the beauty shine through his little eyes.

"Why such feeling in your heart, eh?" Asked the troll looking at the little boy in his hand smiling profusely, "Why this my bounty, this is why I'm here. To watch over this lake for no dwarf can get to it. Dwarves are some of the greediest little rats to be born from the gods, and it is my duty to not let this lake dry up because of them."

"Are those... crystals?" Asked Ahlifer eyes aglow from the magnificent scene before him.

"Aye. The waters produce them, they grow from it."

"Why are you protecting them?"

The troll never asked himself that question, it was just in his nature he always thought. It made him a little perplexed to someone else asking it.

The troll set Ahlifer down on the ground this time, and started walking closer to the edge of the cliff, and closer to the bountiful lake of crystals.

"Follow. I will let you see," said the troll.

The troll looked down at the little boy he'd just met, his shadow stretching over his. He saw the mesmerizing glow in Ahlifer's eyes from the lake full of liquids of crystal.

One tree molded of gold stood tall in the middle. In middle of the forest, a lake full of treasure was — Ahlifer thought bewildered by the sight he had seen.

He felt as if he was in his own personal story, or that he was imagining this whole expenditure of wealth before him. He expostulated with his mind on whether he should trust this new friend of his, the troll.

"What's your name?" Asked Ahlifer out of the blue.

"My name?"

"Yes, your name. Do you have one?"

"Not that I know of," said the troll confused by what a name might be. "Am I supposed to?"

"What is the name of this lake?" Asked Ahlifer ignoring the trolls reply.

"The dwarves call it Grimgar Lake."

"I'll call you Grimgar then," smiled Ahlifer still staring out into the deep crystallized lake.

The troll looked at the little boys smiling face feeling a sense of kindness and an unusual growth of friendship. The troll never had friends, nor a family, leaving his posterity at a dwindling end, and Ahlifer didn't know that; he thought if therw was one troll, there'd be others.

The troll had only one birthright, and expectation living among the living, and that was to guard the treasured lake for whatever reason. Grimgar didn't know why, but he felt as if that was his priority, and main destiny for his rubbish life.

The two new companions kept their quiet and admired the glowing lake full of crystals. Ahlifer never would have guessed he would see such a marvel—but he did, and he didn't want to leave it, and maybe that's why the troll didn't want to leave it, for the obscure and translucent glow that shines from each crystal seduced the brains of the living as if it were an inanimate siren.

Ahlifer was at the point of not trusting his mind for the recents of being cursed by an unknown mad man, to his overreactive imagination made a deadly duo for his current state.

The night was closing in and Grimgar stood up hoisting himself by a tree that laid curved next to the lake. Ahlifer wide eyed looked up to the large troll in thoughts of where his new friend would be going, but he didn't say anything and stayed next to the lake continuing to be seduced by the shiny illumination of the underbelly—the lake.

The gold started to disappear from the tree slowly fading as the shadows of the suns departure began. Ahlifer wiped his eyes in exhaustion, and gave a big yawn goodnight to the days gone.

Ahlifer laid on his belly by the lakeside. He could not sleep. Grimgar slept in near two big boulder next to the large mounting cliff that hung over them; he slept, snoring loudly echoing through the forest line.

Crickets chirped to the night sky, and fireflies hummed around the Crystal Lake blending in with the glow. The lake was peaceful and glowed of white light during the eve which made it a peaceful slumber for Ahlifer.

The next morning, Ahlifer was awoken to the singing of Grimgar — his newly appointed name. The song was not in the language Ahlifer was used to, but the tune of it captured his attention.

It sounded familiar he thought, something related him to the melodic tune; it could have been the monotonous tone of the troll, or the pedantic strange words used in the song.

He wiped the sleep from his eyes and walked over to Grimgar who sat next to a tree that he used to carve markings into it. Odd symbols and shapes and letters were etched into the brown bark from the knife made of stone the troll used.

Grimgar straight faced looked at the groggy boy in pleasure but did not show any emotion — trolls usually had no emotion to begin with, and this lonely troll was not an exception.

He only had his thoughts out in the dense forest, and those thoughts were his only companion for years' time. He was an old troll, smug faced, crows feet to the ears, and the long blunt nose showed it.

His skin was pale, and stretched, with his legs long as a tower. Ahlifer was but a field mouse to him, and the intimidation of Grimgar's height did not weigh on Ahlifer due to the softness of his heart.

"What are you doing?" Asked Ahlifer watching Grimgar carve into the bark of the giant tree that loomed over the troll's head. Grimgar was tall, but the trees were exceedingly more.

"Writing. Words. Such stuff," he replied, still focused, writing more into the bark. "Trees have been here longer. Trolls use them to carry messages to the next. Hollow, and full as well as trolls."

"Are there more trolls around here?" Asked Ahlifer.

"No, just I. When I die, my soul gives life to a new one through the lake. There is never two in these parts, but only one, just like humans, they think they are numbered, but they all share the same life, it what I gathered from the last human I met."

Ahlifer stood quietly pondering what the old troll

meant. Only one human sharing the same life. The words were perplexing, but he did not want to question the troll's intellectual gatherings.

The troll met another human before, and that's what made Ahlifer more intrigued. Was he not the only human in these lands? Maybe he wasn't, and it could possibly lead him to finding out more of how he got there.

"Who was this human you've met before?"

"Woman dressed in fur. Looked like you and such, same nose."

Same nose? Looked like him? Could it have been his sister? Maybe? He didn't think so. But he also didn't know where she was either, and assumed she was still in the village with his father, or was she? He didn't even know where his own mind was until now, so how would he fully know his sister's whereabouts.

Ahlifer uneasy with Grimgar's statement, asked something less twisting in his stomach, "why are you the only troll?"

"Why so many damned questions?" Laughed the troll finally showing emotion. "Humans and their questions. Questioning everything! Be like us trolls and piss away those questions, and just be content with where you are now, the present," the troll then turned his face, "But I do know you are lost, and so I will tell you. Only troll, always have been, look at the trees and it tells me the story of other trolls. I'm carving of what the future trolls will see, so they can learn." *Meet human woman. Now human boy. I'm hungry. Ox is good. Eat the ox. I have a name. Grimgar.*

Ahlifer didn't question more, he felt embarrassed by the constant questions once he thought about it. Grimgar was not used to company, unless it were angry dwarves who travelled through his forest. Ahlifer watched him etch into the tree the symbols, the stories he wrote for the future of his kin. It was the only thing the troll had to communicate with, and it wasn't to communicate with any thing in front of him—he was lonely and Ahlifer saw it in his dark eyes, and he was too.

Ahlifer dreamt of the times back home, wherever it was; he imagined Inga and him still bustling around the dock trying to catch the fish that pulled him in, but this time he didn't fall in, instead they brought it back to their little house and ate it— Mother too, still alive, hard to make out her face, but the soft hands he remembered were there, cutting ripe mid-summer vegetables, squashes, everything of the like. The dream passed by into nothingness, he felt alone again once more.

.

Young was I once, I walked alone,
And bewildered seemed in the way;
Then I found me another and rich I thought me,
For man is the joy of man.

-Hávamál

<u>18</u>

  The broken piece of the boat served well to a point, despite it not being curved correctly to catch a lot of the water, it made do to get the two to the shores before the sun fall. The beaches were filled with rocks, gigantic rocks that steeped all the way to the clouds.

  Golden sand, warm to the touch, and frozen rivers making their way back out the ocean. A waterfall, high and sparkling held high right above them, some of it's water freezing into sharp icicles, while the rest of it down poured right over half of a cave.

  The two made their way from the remainder of what they called a boat. Inga threw the oar and the broken wood aside, quickly rushing towards the warmer sand. Despite it being below freezing, the sand stayed warm; maybe because giants roamed the lands, staying still, watching the oceans— no giants were around right then, so they made took that as an advantage, building a shelter under a cove next to the cave.

They made their steps silent, they both never dealt with the Giants of Jotunheim before, they did not know if they could hear them, more so a mouse. Inga started a fire, hoping it would warm her up more, to maximum temperature, she did not know what the temperature would be like when the Sun completely fell, but a fire would provide the warmth if needed.

"Jotunheim isn't what I expected," sniffled Ratatoskr silently.

"You never been here?" Said Inga moving tinder around for the fire to grow.

"Not that I remember. It's cold, but not freezing cold, ya know?"

Inga looked at him and agreed with a nod, she just stayed to herself, trying to stay quiet, strategize, plan, survive— for whatever the night held, she wanted to be ready for it. Ratatoskr instead burrowed himself between to large rocks to finish his acorn.

As the fire started to roar, crackle, and heat up their small area, Inga started again to think off of the moment; she thought of Ahlifer and where he could be, he thought of her Father, Fjorn and his safety. *From a mundane fishing chore to a stay in Jotunheim*, she thought that was pretty humorous, but the same, rightfully depressing. She missed her family, the friends, and her little house.

The fire was still until a huge winding swoop of air bellowed through the tiny cave, it gave the two a hideous chill. The fire managed to stay alit, but not the warmth. The temperature turned to splintering cold, Inga felt cold spikes pierce her open skin; frosted, miniature icicles stuck in her skin as if they were splinters from a tree.

Millions of them burning her skin. She stayed quiet, furiously shaking them off. It did not affect her little furry companion for him being burrowed away from the passing winds.

"Gods, that hurt," Inga said covering up her bare skin with her tunic. "Now Jotunheim makes a lot more sense for me."

Ratatoskr giggled, burrowing himself deeper in between the rocks while Inga huddled next to them away from the winds direction. The two could not sleep, not only of the rising cold, but the winds that roared through the night. Inga laid there dazing at the fire caught again in the memories of her home.

She was never expecting such an instant adventure, especially dealing with the Gods. Being homesick was hard, she had never had to deal with it, she never left her island, her little land of sanctuary, and this was all a new feeling for her that she did not care for it.

"Three hours," said Ratatoskr shivering.

"What?" Inga said still huddled up by the rocks.

"It's been three hours."

"How in the Gods' names do you know that?" She said curiously. There was no way to tell time in the dark, frozen cave, and it sparked her odd that he knew.

"I have counted, my friend. Counted. It has been eleven-thousand second, eleven-fookin'-thousand seconds of unbearable frozen ground," he started to say, "How do you sleep well with a damned tunic? Aren't you cold?"

"Not really, I'm used to the cold," Inga said shivering.

"You are chattering your teeth, shivering."

"I am cold," she said back.

"You just said you are used to the cold!" Ratatoskr said sliding out of his two rocks. "You shiver but you are not cold?"

"It's in the mind, I stop the cold from reaching it,"

Ratatoskr wrinkled his nose in confusion, he did not understand. He touched her skin feeling the cold flesh, he wrinkled his nose once more, "How? You're skin is cold."

"The mind, my squirrel friend. It is only in the mind," she smiled at his furry face as he came closer. She was cold, but she kept him humored by saying she wasn't—maybe to show her courage, her strength; to lessen her depravity and weaknesses.

He burrowed up close to her, in her arms for more warmth believing she was blessed by the Gods or whatever to radiate continuous warmth.

He hoped he would have gotten some that night, but he didn't, the fire gave it to him. Ratatoskr fell fast asleep as soon as he believed it while Inga stayed frozen, shaking from the icy winds that bellowed though the caverns.

The next morning Ratatoskr sprung out of Inga's arms towards the dying campfire while she stayed asleep. He ran around it, waving his tail around in happiness, it was finally warmer, warm enough to carry on with their travels towards the rainbow bridge. The only thing was to get Inga up; she was a hard sleeper, could sleep through the wickedest storms, especially running on no sleep.

He started pushing on her face with his delicate claws, enough to make her sound, she groaned to it in annoyance. Her face cold, frozen, tears chilled in place under her eyes from the night terrors she had. He pushed again with all his might, flapping his tail even harder. She did not move a muscle.

"Are you dead?" Said Ratatoskr huffing and panting still pushing on her frozen face. "Gods! You are dead. You were cold. I knew it," he walked to the fire to grab a little kindling still aflame, he put it on her cold face hoping it would cause a much more immediate reaction than his little claws.

He saw it did not, she just moaned again in her sleep. "At least you seem to be alive," he said again. "The dead usually do not say anything.

Unless you turned into one of them fookin' draugrs. Are you turning into one of them? If you are, warn me. I hate them nasty buggers, the smells of them are the worse. I can't have you stinkin' up this fine cave now."

He continued to ramble to her. If she was awake, or showed any signs of it, she would have hit him on the side of his little fuzzy head right back to the top of Yggdrasil.

The winds didn't help, they still roared through the caves, but unlike the night, it was a little more bearable, more warmer, not like a summer in Svartlheim, but more so a fall in Midghard.

The Sun helped it, warm, bright, making things awaken so they could help contribute their warmth.

Rumblings in the back of the cave sounded as if an earthquake had begun, but unlike most earthquakes usually lasting not more than ten seconds, this one kept going. *A hungry giant's belly?* Ratatoskr thought to himself, *Must be.*

He paid no more attention to the continuous shifting of earth, his mission was to wake his companion up. He jumped on her side, trudging his paws into her side.

"Dear girl, wake the fook up!" He said panicking even more impatiently, "There may be a Giant about to eat us for his dinner, ya damned girl!" He clawed her more viciously this time, piercing her cold skin with his claws, drawing blood. "Too far into the flesh, my apologies. You had it coming. You dragged me all the way to this cold land and then fall asleep, an eternal sleep," he saw the frozen tears again, he stopped his actions looking in more closely, lifting her left eye lid up, her eyes were a frozen blue that covered the whites. "Oh shit, you are dead. Well, shit shit shit," he panicked, threw himself off of her. "I did not see anything, fookin' cold got that one, I will tell them. Tell who? Whoever is concerned I guess," he kept his rambling going. The sounds of the moving earth felt closer, roaring, bellowing, it was no wind.

Ratatoskr dove under the two rocks once more hiding, peering out, scouting to see what it would be that came to them from the depths of the mysterious cave.

His little eyes glistening in fright, hidden under some ice, he saw two tall figures come out of the dark. He cursed himself over and over for not getting her up in time, he cursed her too for being such an oaf.

Giants he saw, two giants came, there skin, mixed of ice and rock and some flesh—an intimidating sight to see. Ratatoskr had never even seen one before, now he wished he didn't.

The reluctant fear that came from them; hideous, monstrous, ugly—their faces came into the light. Stone faces, widened to their shoulders, still ugly, but a little more bearable to lay the eyes on. They walked to the sleeping Inga, setting down tall fishing poles to the side.

"What in the worlds?" Said one giant to the other. His voice of cold and dark replicating the winds that roared the night before. "What is this?" He picked her frozen body up by her leg, dangling her body in front of his giant eye. "One of them ice fiends?"

"Don't be silly. Read a book once and awhile, Gyrolm" said the other. "This is a human, one of the Gods creations."

"Human," the giant referred to Gyrolm said while thinking, "Ah, a human. Why in Jotunheim?"

"I wouldn't know," said his friend. "She's frozen to the bone, maybe she died here quite some time ago. Years maybe."

Gyrolm carefully set her down back to where she

first laid. Ratatoskr breathed heavily from the panic he was induced when laying eyes on the two giants, his tail laid flat on the ground, between the two rocks. They didn't eat her, nor rip her apart... maybe the stories of giants were misleading.

Ratatoskr flew out of the two rocks immediately once the giants had left the cave towards the sea. He felt relieved but still was having a minor panic attack. A little squirrel surrounded by towering giants, bristling with ice was not a good way to spend the day.

"Damn you, Inga. Are you dead?" Said Ratatoskr slapping her face back and forth. Her eyelids flickered as if she was trying to open them, which gave a good sight for the little squirrel. "Can't open your eyes? Well shite!

Inga mumbled some words he could not understand, probably something not important he thought, so he ran to the now dead fire, finding warm kindling that would help unfreeze his friend.

He did it quickly, he did not want the giants to come back and see them two alive; maybe they liked their food alive? He didn't know, or what if they liked the torture of their food? He had to stop thinking and get Inga's eyes open to her surroundings.

He carefully held the glowing stick to her eye lids hoping it would open them up, he was no sage, someone who could wake the dead, if she was dead of course, he hoped she wasn't, she did speak, but do draugrs once and awhile.

He saw more flickering of the eyelids and trembling of her frozen lips, what a good sign indeed he thought. He pressed the stick into her eyelashes trying to set them aflame hoping that would give the frozen areas consistent heat so they can melt away.

"Inga, I feel really sick to my stomach, I do. I feel as if I'm torturing the dead. Should I just bury you? I feel like that would be a better idea, I do."

"No!" Cried Inga instantly, eyes still frozen, slapping the squirrel across the cave. "I can't see! Damn you, squirrel!"

"Damn me? Damn you! Damn you and me for going all the way to this frozen shite hole!" Said Ratatoskr picking himself up and hopping back to her. "I thought you were dead, or to be dead, or to be Giant's food. I would have made a good appetizer, I'd hate that. You would be a good meal though."

"What are you going on about, squirrel?" She said sitting up, eyes frozen shut.

"Ol' Gyrolm and his friend, whom I did not catch his name were most likely going to eat you. You frozen stupid girl. Instead, they went fishing. You got lucky," Ratatoskr went on. "I like fish, I am hungry."

Inga ignored his rant like she has been doing when he went off subject, instead she tried to open her frozen eyelids with her fingers. She felt the nerves tears apart as if they grew together from the ice. Clasped together like a newly sewn linen shirt, it hurt to tear it apart. She cried out in pain, but drowned it out with frustration, grunts of stubbornness.

Ratatoskr on the other hand, ran to the cave's entrance to look where the two giants went, still cursing her for their situation. He wouldn't blame anyone else, his ego was too large for it, that's why he always pitted the Eagle and Nidhug against each other — for pure amusement for himself.

Some would say when the world's shook, it was from Nidhug, the dragon underneath Yggdrasil due to Ratatoskr spreading more lies to him, and his anger would sound the grounds.

"Oi, Stupid girl! Want to go fishing with them Giants?" Said Ratatoskr while looking at them casting their lines out into the large sea. "Fish would be good, beats this cold. Besides, seems to be warmer out there. Who woulda thought?"

Inga was still trying to open her frozen eyes, one was loosening, but the other, not so much. The pain was inconceivable, burning and stinging from the tiny ice that held the eyelids together.

"No, not with giants," she said quietly. "My eyes are shut, help me."

"I have been helping you! I tried to open them, they opened at first, but now frozen shut after one wind came in. Right before the giants," Ratatoskr then popped up right beside her as if he was there the entire time, "Giants! They know this land better than us, anyone, probably even the Gods. Maybe the Gods, I'm not sure. The Aesir are kind of homebodies it seems like."

"Get to it!" Said Inga letting her impatience get the best of her.

"Talk to those ol' giants and maybe they know how to open your eyes. Not metaphorically speaking, but I'm sure they could open your eyes in a sense where you could see again."

Inga stopped forcing her eyelids open. Not a bad idea she thought, but could go bad. She didn't know the temperaments of Giants, more so the whole idea of letting a Giant doctor her up. Her eyes were stinging, eyelids and all — nothing else to do, so the two gathered there stuff and went to the Oceanside where the fishing giants mingled together.

"Giant kind!" Yelled Ratatoskr towards them trying to draw their attention, but they did not hear. He ran closer forgetting the blinded Inga behind him. She walked around holding out her frozen hands trying to find her way. "I said Giant kind! Giant race! Giants! Fookin' Giants!" He kept going.

They continued to fish, Gyrolm baiting his line with a fish the size of a human, notching it to a largely placed hook. The other giant looked back, head staying mounted on his shoulders, swiveling his body to match the little squirrel running towards them.

"By old King Pjazi, a squirrel," said the Giant. Gyrolm turned his body still rod in hand seeing the squirrel running up to them. They could not make out what he was saying, but his mouth moved faster than any sea serpent they had ever seen.

"A squirrel? Here? So far south?" Said Gryolm immensely confused, "first a human, now a squirrel. Today is odd it is." He set his pole down turning his whole body towards the yipping squirrel who was running full speed at him.

Ratatoskr courageously leaped onto Gryolm's head. The old Giant didn't even wince at it, he just spun in circles trying to find him. Dizzy he was, his friend stopped him in his tracks, mid-motion. He stopped raising his icy eyes towards the sky spotting Ratatoskr's tail swinging down his brow.

"What you doing up there, squirrel?" Said Gyrolm patiently as ever.

"My friend is frozen. She can't see correctly. Ya' might know what to do, right?" Said Ratatoskr bending down, perched on his forehead. "I mean, you are used to the cold, right?"

"Of course we are, it's Jotunheim. What we aren't used to is this warm weather, humans and squirrels here down the south," said Gryolm. "What are you doing here?"

Ratatoskr opened his mouth about to tell the giant of what they were doing, until he remembered, if he told the Giants they were going to Asgard, they wouldn't take kindly of that. Allies of the Aesir, meant death to those allies.

He thought of the many violent deaths he could face if he told them of where they were heading. He chose to ignore it, point his tiny little paw towards his blind friend, Inga still frozen to the core walking in wide circles trying to find her way.

"She's frozen. Eyes shut cold. Anyway way to open them?" Ratatoskr said perching himself back down to the giant.

"Yes," started the other Giant, "Back in town, but the problem is, we are fishing. You must wait for us to be done," there was the stubbornness the Ice Giants of Jotunheim were profoundly known of. "Ten Silver Gills, then we can go back," he said again.

Ratatoskr weighed out his options, his snarky replies, but he had no choice but to do what they said, for he was the guest in Jotunheim and guests in Jotunheim had to wait for their host. He cursed himself again, "Damn these giants," he said it in his head, not to loud he hoped. Never could tell if he said things out loud or in his head.

"Fine," he agreed.

19

It was morning once again, sun aching one, burning their minds and foreheads. Boulder's Edge was known for its hot temperatures. The city was built around rocks that collected the heat of The Sun exasperating the energy around the city and its landscapes.

Tillu and Edvar galloped softly through the woods. The woods were livened by the birds, the frogs, the rustling of leaves that fell from the trees.

They paid no mind of where they were, just as they kept following the trail towards the town where they could set sail for Vosno.

They were quiet among each other, no talking of the escape. They stole some horses from Krevii's men and then started their travels knowing not where they were going. Edvar stole some haunches of boar meat, he could not ride on an empty stomach, and he sat proudly on the horse while it galloped through the dried leaves chewing loudly on a leg. "My favorite part of this adventure is you stealing boar," said Tillu looking over at his bald friend. "Hand me some, I'm hungry."

"Damned good boar too," said Edvar digging in a stolen knapsack full of stolen meat.

He handed his friend a charred haunch, still a little warm from the leather bag that kept it that way. Tillu took a reluctant bite bringing in all of the smell of flavor, he let out a huge joyful sigh. They had not eaten since they had left their village, good timing for Edvar to use the brain he had left that worked.

Edvar threw the meatless bone in satisfaction to the side of the road. He was full now, when he was filled to the brim, it was time for some mead.

Luckily he had a stolen jug of mead, he pulled it out happily, chugging the whole thing dry. Tillu looked over at him in complete disbelief at the ambiguous now empty jug.

Stole mead too?" Tillu laughed, "Save any for me?"

"Not this jug, got more," he said with a smile. "They are for later, celebration. When we get to the boats, we steal one, then we can drink."

Tillu shook his head again with the same laughter. They kept riding, deeper down the trail. They were probably ten paces out by now from where Krevii's camp was.

Tillu kept his guard hoping they weren't being followed by a patrol, or spotted by a scout, they were on stolen horses of a Jarl which would be the penalty of death if ever caught.

Not to mention the fact that Edvar stole a week's supply of boar and mead. They kept their pace, slowly, but steadily galloping at a fair speed through the woods.

"Stop where you're going horse riders!" Sounded a deep voice through the woods, "You are on property of Jarl Krevii!"

Not knowing where the voice came from and startled by it, they kicked their horses to full speed, gliding through the forest.

Thunderous sounds came from all sides of the forest, horses, many of them to equal a Jarl's raiding party. They wondered why so many, they had no time to keep thinking, they had to focus, to keep the horses on the road.

"Just our luck!" Said Edvar galloping fast trying to tighten the stolen knapsack. "Do you think they came for the mead and haunches?"

Tillu laughed under his breath to his burly friend, he couldn't reply, the wind swept making it hard to talk. Edvar didn't care about the wind, he cared more about the celebratory mead and his food. They raced and raced feeling arrows start to whiz by their heads.

"Trying to kill us! Damn them," said Edvar slowing his pace down. Tillu looked back to his friend decreasing his speed, he did the same. He didn't want to die right now and knowing Edvar's thick skull, he had a plan of some sort.

He wouldn't have just halted his movement for no reason, especially when his death was right next to him, but death wasn't a good friend of his, his scars of axes and blades on his skull proved just that.

The roaring of galloping stopped and the neighing of horses were only sounded. Edvar got off his horse in a sign of surrender. He didn't want to surrender though, again his skull proves he never usually does. He stuck his hands up laughing; he usually did that to mock the enemy, or because it was all too humorous for him. Tillu pulled right next to him getting off his horse as well pulling out the axe he had stolen from Krevii's camp.

To the right and to the left, they were caved in by Krevii's men, each carrying a symbol of the Jarl's insignia on their shields. They moved in closer to them, the front shielding up, the back, men with swords, sharp, glistened in The Sun that pierced through the canopies of the forest.

"Sudden stop for such fools," said a man coming out of the shields, "Why did you run?" It was Krevii, the Jarl himself with a face of empathy.

"We weren't running," said Edvar. "that's why we stopped, did you forget sumthin'?"

"Trying to cross the ocean?" Said Krevii ignoring Edvar's sarcastic antics. "Why?"

Edvar kept his quiet with a smile hoping Tillu would speak up, even though Tillu didn't know what else to say, especially after this partial surrender, he just put his axes back in his lash.

They were still surrounded, but Krevii made it apparent by the way he walked up to them that he wasn't looking for a fight, instead he just grabbed Edvars knapsack off his horse and dug through it to see what they took.

"Mead and haunches of boar?" Said Krevii with a slight confused smile, "that's why you ran?"

"No, not really," immediately said Edvar embarrassed, "It was just for the road."

"Road for where?"

"Road to some place that I can not member'," said Edvar scratching his deepest scar on his bald head trying to show him that his brain was probably scrambled.

"Where were you guys going?" Said Krevii again now looking at Tillu.

"We were going to the sea," Tillu admitted, but still standing his ground. "Hoping we could get a ship to the East."

Krevii had his men lower their own guard giving Tillu and Edvar a little more peace of mind to explain their situation. It helped for the most part, but Tillu still was suspicious; a man they thought was mad now talking to them as another brother.

Edvar put his hands down sighing in relief to all of it. He knew his plan was going to work, his plan being just to talk and reason. For a barbarous man, that was odd, but Edvar after all those blows to the head, his actions were always pretty unpredictable.

"Why the ocean?" Said Krevii still confused on why they left so suddenly.

"Ullfr, why did we see him a couple of days ago, but you say you killed him?" said Tillu now taking charge hoping to get some kind of answers. "Do you understand that isn't possible right?"

Krevii looked down smiling to himself a frustrated smile. He now felt as if he was dealing with two mad men who just raided his camp, seeking a long forgotten city, bent on their sleepless minds.

He didn't give them the satisfactions of answering, to him it wouldn't have done anyone good trying to explain who he is, and what Boulder's Edge was. Instead, he signaled two of his men to grab them, their horses and to bring them back to camp.

Tillu bashed around while they tied his hands together like some rabid animal. Edvar stayed calm, drunkenly calm, which was strange for him, usually when he was drunk, he was more volatile.

They were hauled on horseback, tied around the feet and their hands. Tillu cursed himself for being captured, to even listening to Edvar and his plan. Half way's mark to the port to make their way by boat to Vosno and to be captured by the same men they were fleeing, how tragic Tillu especially though.   They rode in between two groups of men; the warriors in the back had long oak bows, while in the front, they carried weapons of steel—axes, swords, spears. Edvar looked at Tillu from the side of his horse laughing, Tillu didn't appreciate his drunken friend finding amusement in the situation, and he ignored him letting him laugh to himself.

They were both not good at this, there was always a third to help, Fjorn being the third. Fjorn's mind was a mind no other mortal mind could match, especially in these particular events, but again, Fjorn was no where, could have been dead for all they knew.

The Sun was giving its way, falling down to the edges of Midghard, trees letting in the last of its shine. Bird's scuttling through the tree branches with squirrels that ran up trees. The sounds all became to present for the racing mind of Tillu.

He did not know if they were being rode into their execution, the strange reactions of Krevii left it a mystery. Stolen provisions from a Jarl, stolen horses, usually meant immediate death for the suspects.

"Jarl," said Tillu speaking to Krevii showing a kind gesture of giving him his title.

"Yes?" Said Krevii spinning his head behind him towards Tillu.

"We will talk, yes?" Said Tillu with a slight demand, "We aren't headed for execution, right?"

Krevii turned his head back on the road giving him no answer which gave Tillu an uncomfortable feeling in his stomach.

Edvar on the other hand was still laughing, swaying drunkenly on his horse; if he was going to die, he wanted to die laughing, drunk and happy. There was something else though, Tillu couldn't figure it out.

A brigand this big, to search them out for mere stolen haunches of boar and a couple bottles of mead, there was something else, but he could not put his finger on it.

Krevii had a secret, a secret to all this madness, Tillu knew and deep down in Edvar's sober subconscious, he also knew. They had to play the captors now, stay silent, until further orders were said.

So close to the port, so close to a safe haven, so close to escape, now bundled in ropes heading back to a camp they never wanted to go back to.

<u>20</u>

Misty now, Grimgar was singing a song in a tongue Ahlifer couldn't understand. He liked the sound to it, it was peaceful, relaxing. For everything he has been through in the past days, it felt like a medicine to his mind, much needed, and Grimgar knew that.

A Forest Troll, one of the last in the worlds of Svartlheim, the land of the dwarves; stories were told of his race were scratched into a tall tree, strange characters represented the alphabet they used showing they were born with language.

"What does this say?" Said Ahlifer pointing at a small sentence on the bark.

"Dwarves like treasure more than life," said Grimgar reluctantly stopping his song. "Dwarves like the lake, where we are born. They think its treasure, but its life to us. We are born to protect it."

Ahlifer was fascinated by the lake that glistened.

Giving life to an intelligent race was very peculiar but rose the curiosity of anyone. For the Dwarves, they saw it as treasure, while the Troll's saw it as a Mother of sorts, a breeding life.

But what was there purpose? Thought Ahlifer. There is a purpose to everything. For him, it was to live for the Gods, to the Troll it was to write?

"You were born out of that lake, right?" Said Ahlifer again.

"Yes, we all are. The trolls."

"So, what is your purpose to life?" Said Ahlifer still trying to grasp the nature of his new friend, "You are born from the lake, then what? Do you just climb this cliff to write on the tree? How do you know it's up here? Have you been to the cities? The villages? Why remain in this forest?"

Grimgar had never been questioned of his own nature. To him, it was just how it was, how he felt, how the past trolls felt.

He thought hard about it, he did not know how to answer to the little human boy. He scratched his head touching the words on the bark, concentrating on them.

"I guess I never looked at it that way, little human. We usually don't."

"When you say *we*, you mean your ancestors, correct?" Said Ahlifer, "As in the ones before?"

"Yes, the ones before me, we never name ourselves too," continued Grimgar moving his giant finger along the words on the bark, carefully studying them even more. "We are to serve the Lake, our Mother. The crystals give us life," he repeated.

"Yes, I know, you told me that," said Ahlifer patiently. "Look, I was born, given a name, I grow old, die, go to the Gods. There are stories of legends, stories of tales and such, but that's it."

Grimgar became even more confused of all the new information. He scratched his chest this time, pressing his hand down on it afterward to feel his heart beat.

All creatures have hearts he knew, maybe that was a significant detail. He took a stone in his hands to write it down next to his verses for the future trolls, *I have a heart, so does everything that lives.*

Ahlifer watched him carve the words into the bark. He could not read them, but when he saw the sadness over Grimgar's face, he could tell he was the one who caused it. Ahlifer didn't know what else to say, there wasn't. He saw the troll exhausted by everything he had said, even a little sad from the big brows that curved to his eyes.

"Look, Grimgar. I was just only asking what it was like to be one of your kind," said Ahlifer trying to apologize. "I didn't mean to upset you."

"Ragnarok," said the troll wiping away the sad expression off his face, turning it into a fiercer one. "Ragnarok will come, the tree will stay, and this will be what will be left of this old world."

Ahlifer became uneasy with it. He knew of Ragnarok, the battle between the Gods, brothers fighting brothers, a never ending winter, and the world burning. He just never thought of it as if it was tomorrow.

The curse upon him marked something, the voice that led him here, maybe to learn more about the final act of this world.

"How does Ragnarok happen again? How did it start? You know, right?" Said Ahlifer nervously.

"We Forest Trolls are the scribes of this land, only

131

this land. I do not know how it will start, but it will be The Fool who starts it," he said reading more.

"The Fool?" Said Ahlifer. "Loki?" Ahlifer went to his memory for the educations of the sagas, he learned them when he was young, but only saw them as tales, not actual events. He remembered where he was, in front of a troll, in the land of Dwarves—maybe the tales were true. The Voice that led him here, could it have been something to do with the end times?

"Deep thought, sometimes good, boy. Don't stay in your mind too long though, it will turn into an enemy of what you can't control," said Grimgar still studying the words on the tree.

The voice led him here, Ahlifer knew that, but why? Did it want him to learn, to retreat, why was he here? It wasn't the lake, it wasn't to meet Grimgar, nor see his first Dwarf drink a bottle of ale to himself, there was something more. Ahlifer started walking back to the dead morning fire, gathering needed supplies for his continuing journey.

"Leaving?" Said Grimgar with a slight smile.

"I have to find out why I'm here," said Ahlifer.

"As do I, boy. As do I."

Both, born and to die, but the middle they had to figure out themselves. Stopping the circling motion of life then death, life then death, and so on.

Learning from each other, they knew there was a bigger reason, not a natural one, but something they could both do. It was their own saga, an unwritten tale, an unsung ballad, all that consisted in their own minds and actions.

As Ahlifer was packing up some essentials, mostly given to him by Grimgar, he noticed one black bird, a raven peering down to him from a branch that bent low from the Tree of Words.

Usually ravens would leave from the sight of humans, but this one did not. He gave out a deep croak and then fluttered off as soon as Ahlifer turned away from it. Very odd, he thought to himself.

Grimgar walked over to Ahlifer reaching out his hand towards him; he held an outfit out of bark, as if they were meant for armor. It came with a large shield, the size of Ahlifer himself, but was very light for him, with a strap for around his back. Ahlifer put all of it on right away, he felt like a little log, but not as heavy as one.

"Thank you," he said to Grimgar.

"You go north now, boy. That is where you'll find more of us, they will know more."

"More of you? I thought you said you were just one of the one?" Ask Ahlifer.

"In the South, yes, North, no. Forest Scribes are everywhere, not just trolls Woodland Trolls such as I. Different shapes and sizes."

Ahlifer gave a hug around the troll's giant hand giving Grimgar a new feeling, something more he needed in his life; hope and understanding, love and compassion, something his ancestors never got to experience.

Ahlifer clunked in his tree armor off down the trail towards the town he first woke up in. It would lead him to the north, traveling some where he did not know.

He had no choice but to trust his conscience at this time, he couldn't figure out why he was leaving, but when Grimgar talked more of Ragnarok, the more he felt he had to do something about it, to proceed onward. So he did.

The Raven earlier gave him an odd feeling, a sense of something greater looking over him. It was an anxious feeling at that, but there was something else to. He didn't know what birds lived among the Dwarven Lands, seeing a familiar one gave him comfort.

But what was the Raven doing out here? He thought. Why did it look to me as if it knew who I was? He knew the difference of animals' sights; when they look at you when you are closing down on them in a hunt, this one didn't feel like that, it felt like somebody knew as well.

Ahlifer, in the armor made of bark made his way towards the Crystal Lake, to see it for himself. He wanted to touch it — it was his adventure after all, his journey home, but on the way there, he had to learn of the upcoming threats that shrouded in the misty borders of each of the worlds.

Nine worlds, he's been to two of them. He laughed to that thought. He never thought the stories to be true, but here he was, in Svartlheim itself.

He was a little ways away from Grimgar's hearth, when two dwarf's dressed in armor approached him. They looked at him, dressed in bark as if it were a joke. They laughed at it, stroking their long grizzly beards in enjoyment. Ahlifer paid no attention to them, he just stopped, waited for a reply from them.

"We saw you at Rhyvens Inn couple days back," laughed one of the dwarves.

"Now in bark clothing," laughed the other.

Ahlifer didn't feel as if he should continue talking to them, they were less important, so he kept walking towards town. He pounded of wood every time he took a step forward.

The two dwarves turned around laughing at him as he kept clanking down the stony road. Dwarves were proud creatures, that's what damned them from the start; focused on their ego and their gold, it left them weak in the end.

The road felt long, especially dressed up as a tree. Ahlifer didn't want to take the armor off, it was warm. It also covered his mangy tunic that he'd been dressed in since his drowning. Although embarrassment was never an occurring feeling for him, he felt a little awkward, especially in a whole world that had not a single human in it.

When he reached Rhyvens Inn it was late afternoon, the evening sun doing its role, slipping lower into the land. Dwarves in the plaza all looked at him as he opened the door to the Inn, mostly a tavern, but Inn gave it a better ring to it. No one really stayed there, maybe the drunkards who fell out mid drink of their mead, but other than that it was a place of drink and song after a hard days work in the mountains.

When he opened the door, he expected to be crowds like the first time. This time there was only two or three dwarves sitting in high chairs? They looked at him with the same looks as he did in the plaza. He just trudged through the bar towards the keep, who sat on the other side of the smaller sized table.

"Bar keep," nodded Ahlifer.

"Tree boy," nodded the barkeep back. "What will you have today?"

"Not looking for anything. Just wanted to talk," said Ahlifer.

The Bar Keep looked curious at him, staring down his attire made of a tree.

"This outfit is from a good friend. It is weird at first, yes, but imagine it as plates of steel," said Ahlifer trying to get to his point, "I woke up here, did you see me when I stayed asleep in the booth back there?"

"I don't remember ye' but maybe my Mammy would know. Her eyes are full of sight, even a Giant's don't pair," said the Dwarf walking to the back room. "Oi Mammy!" He bellowed.

Ahlifer sat comfortably at the table patiently waiting for this Mammy to come talk to him. The patrons still eyeing him down saying nothing. He became a little nervous of his slight bravery, he never really could do the talking without his sister.

An old frail old Dwarf, as tall as Ahlifer came walking out of the back room, brews in hand for the other guests. Her eyes glossy showing her slight blindness. Ahlifer was then filled with doubt. How would a blind old lady recall the events of him waking up in the tavern? He mustered his courage instead.

"You need me?" She said with a voice that matched her figure. "Need a drink?"

"Boy wants to know if you ever seen him in Rhyvens?" Said the other Dwarf.

"About two nights ago, I woke up here, in that booth," Ahlifer said while pointing out the exact spot he woke from a coma like slumber.

Mammy wriggled her eyebrows adjusting her sight to see the young boy, who was now dressed in a bark attire. She came out around the table towards him, still adjusting her eyes, wriggling her brows up and down slowly. When she came closer Ahlifer's stomach filled with anxiousness.

"Why are you in a tree?" She asked.

"Met a troll out in the woods."

"A troll? The lake one? Full of them shiny crystals?" She asked.

Ahlifer nodded not knowing if it were a good idea to tell her more about Grimgar. Dwarves were greedy according to Grimgar's ancestral writings. He didn't want anything to harm him.

"I mean, no. Sort of. There was a lake," he reluctantly said.

She set the cups of drink onto the table in front of

him. Both filled to the brim with their home brewed mead they kept in the back. She slid one over to him to show the hospitality the Inn was all about. She took a sip from her own cup, then waved for the other dwarf to leave so the two could chat.

"Drink," she said coughing on her drink. "It will help to talk."

Ahlifer took a sip of the harsh mead, choking on its bitterness. His face warmed up, his muscles tingled, and his tongue coated with honey.

He liked the taste, even though strong, the honey cooled the alcohol down as if he never drank it in the first place.   "Did you see me two nights ago?" He asked wiping away the remainder of the mead from his upper lip. "I woke up here… in my tunic," he showed her it underneath the bark.

"Aye, I may be going blind, but I seen you sitting there, then rustling out like a chicken hatched right out of an egg. I don't know where you came from, but you stayed here for most the time. Kept quiet, only murmured to yourself in your sleep."

"What was I saying?" He asked.

"I didn't pay no attention, just saw your lips move, mumbling and so forth to yourself."

The voice, he was talking to the voice, he knew it. Knowing that much would put him on track. To go where from here was the bigger question. No leads besides the illusive ghost. It stopped speaking to him ever since he woke up. He remembered the terrible sound of it though, laughing in amusement to his pleas. He needed to find it again. He hated that, but he did.

"Thanks Mammy," said Ahlifer standing up from his seat. "I have to go now."

"The troll. I want to hear more about it," she said eyes growing wider. "You seeing the myth yourself brings me hope."

The legend of the troll, known to Ahlifer as Grimgar was a mythical creature out in the untouchable forests. No Dwarves besides the fathers of their fathers had ever seen it, then the young lost human boy who miraculously wound up in Svartlheim.

Ancient tales told of it, such as the heroic ballads of Giants and Men in Midghard.

He smiled at her giving her the respect she deserved; she did show the hospitality he longed for, the gratuitous acts of kindness as well. He told her the story that moment, everything, from the tree of words, to the Crystal Lake that the troll was born from. He saw the glimmer of her childhood dreams grow in her heart, her hazy eyes, the sparkles of happiness and warmth.

He trusted her that she would not tell anyone else of Grimgar and she wouldn't tell a single soul from that moment forward, nor Gufnir who stayed in the shadowy booth where he first met Ahlifer.

"I shall keep your secret as well human," he took a huge sip of his mead, slamming down to the table. He now wearing royal colors, "The King of Dwarves will always have your back."

21

The volva, beautiful seers that knew the future of the worlds, always keeping it a secret from the secrets of living things; only the trees, birds, wolves would congregate with them, hearing their messages, but never ask.

They ate what the earth ate, they drank from the world's oceans and lakes, rivers and waterfalls.

Sajja was the eldest of the three shamans, volva's who maintained a friendship in the woods on the world of Midghard. Face of pale white, with tattoos of runic symbols even Heimdall could not read.

She and her sisters belonged to the wolves, the White Wolf, Odin's favorite he sent for his own reasons to Midghard.

They kept out of sight with the mythical wolf by their side from the mortals, keeping the balance between the God's and humans.

Humans would want their secrets, violently search, and extort them, so the mystical veil shrouded the three and its animals from the sights deep in the woods on the edges of the small fishing village of Thor's Heart.

Drums organically deep, livening up the little woods with the sounds of their preserved life. Sajja and her sisters, Illen and Yujl played on them, beating to the rhythm of the winds, welcoming Mani, the moon to their existence for another night.

Darkness blended, fought with the fire while the winds trembled among the branches stirring the atmosphere into a dark one. Someone was coming through the veil, a God, an Aesir, whatever be it it startled the three sisters.

"Who breaks through *Runsa*?" Called out Sajja referring to the magical barrier. "Aesir, what do you want?" She said again hoping to get an answer.

The bushes shook from whoever was approaching. The seers stopped their drums, calming the winds to hear out more. Sajja picked up a small dagger made of enchanted steel. She pierced her eyes into the dark bush line awaiting for the figure to approach.

"Just I, the good ol' Fool," smiled Loki while wiping off his tunic. "I hear you ladies could tell me my future? Or do I need to cut a giants head off? I mean, I could."

Sajja lowered the dagger throwing it to the

ground. She looked at him in disgust. She hated him. His egotistic, cynical mind made the job hard for the seers, especially the fates of its counterparts.

Seeing he in Midghard also made her upset and the fact he had searched them out. Aesir's were never supposed to be involved with them, nor communicate directly and it made her upset even more.

"Your future is your own, Loki," said Sajja, her lips curling.

"See, I don't like to read books, I like to skip to the end," he laughed, "Tell me. What do you know of my death?"

"We know as much as you when the Volva of Yggdrasil told Odin."

He laughed, brushing his long blonde hair to the side of his ears and then coldly looking into Sajja's eyes again, "Odin does not share everything. Especially with me."

"I couldn't imagine," Sajja said back still firmly eyeing him down.

"They are after me, probably going to kill me, or what not, but you know this right?"

Sajja stayed still not letting him manipulate his way into her own knowledge. She kept her stance, shoulders up, eyes stiff.

He walked closer to her, sitting himself down by the open fire that lit up the part of the forest they dwelled in. He touched it, feeling the heat burn his skin. He giggled.

"Fire hurts even on Midghard," he smiled looking at his burnt finger. "Anyway, not really the point. I need to know where a good exit route is, where will I end up where I won't die. You can tell me that."

"I can not," said Sajja firmly.

Loki closed his eyes in frustration still holding his finger. He was impatient, such as he was all the time, but this time with his life on the line, he was more demanding.

The Aesir were after him, once they catch him, he would be tortured to death, and he knew that. His patience and life relied on the Volvas of the worlds, mainly of Midghard.   "I can not go to any of the sisters, but you three," he started to explain.

"We aren't easily bendable," replied

Sajja.   "Not even close. You are full of wisdom, I'll give you that. You know humans and their minds more than us Aesir."

"You are not an Aesir, but a Giant who slid his way in the halls."

Loki was getting more frustrated as time went on. He needed their wisdom but his desperate actions were becoming too much a weakness. His time was running short, he knew that. The three sisters knew it as well. Holding their tongues from such was a pact they signed when being born by the cosmos.

Loki slid his burnt hand again over the fire feeling the warming touch burn his hand even more. He shuttered to the pain this time, not laughing. Sajja looked at him with a confused face. He looked at her as he hovered his hand over the fire, biting his lip. She turned her head to her sisters seeing if they were as surprised as her.

"Why do you burn your hand?" She asked. "What are you trying to prove?"

"The pain of burning flesh, it hurts us and humans," he said as he clenched his hurting hand into his other, "Us *divine* do feel pain, but humans endure it more, they let it get to them, sly right into their minds. Emotions they call it. I saw it first hand," he stopped in silence, "I do not know where to go. A boy I had talked to as an apparition of his own death. I saw his death. Why can't I see mine?"

The three sisters hovered around the fire where Loki tended to his tinged hand. He looked at them as they circled around him.

He saw Sajja stick her nose out sniffing the winds, the burned flesh, and the nature that danced around them. She touched his hand, then blew on it with a dust of magical property. He felt the pain disappear.

"Fool, Svartalfar holds more than us here in Midghard. That is all I well tell you," said Sajja.

The other two sisters disappeared into the darkness, escaping the light of the fire. Sajja stood out, eyes aglow with whole crystal blue colors. Her lips cold as the winter.

Now in a trance of binding with her surroundings. She looked into the future of Midghard for any truth of why he was here and where it would lead. Nothing.

Loki stood up wiping his hands on his tunic. He smiled at her as she stayed still glowing. He knew she was finally giving in. He saw the flicker of the flames trigger her blue glossy eyes. For once he felt comfort — panic dissipating away.

Her eyes flickered, her mouth wriggled. She was seeing something she had never seen when looking into the future. He knew that right when the first tear shed down her cheek.

"Selfishness," Sajja said, "You have awoken the end of times, Loki."

"What do you mean?" Asked Loki, "Awoken the end?"

"Yes," said Sajja again, eyes now full of tears, "The worlds are coming to an end."

Sajja led out a deep bellow of sadness, tears came pouring out of her eyes. She felt the pain of her world, the suffering of it's inhabitants. Whatever she saw, it was Loki's doing. She collapsed onto the ground crying. The pain she felt was unimaginable.

Loki looked at her lying on the ground rolling around in agony. He remembered the pain he felt from the fire — the pain that now flew into the sky, swirling with green flames. He trembled, but stayed confident that he still had a chance to undo his own fate. He was too high and mighty to think nonetheless.

"The fire burns your mind," he said picking her up, "Just like a human, you feel it."

He set her on a straw bed inside a tent. Loki was curious on how she felt the whole world and only its pain. He wondered if it was really coming to an end.

If so, he would not allow himself to end with it. He had to find someone or something that would help further. The boy, he thought, what if he talked to the boy again.

To go back to taking him as a hostage — a fragile, weakened mind could help him buy more time even Odin wouldn't dare seek him out.

The boy's father was now in the hands of Sultr, claimed by him and his army of fire. Loki set that up. Odin's willing to know was also used as a downfall for him and he knew that, so that's why he travelled to Muspelheim right before taking control of Ahlifer.

A mere distraction that played out well, he thought, but now maybe controlling the mind of another human would be beneficial in this time of need.

"Rest now, woman. The end will come soon enough," Loki smiled while leaving the Volva's camp back into the darkness of the forest, onward to find the boy from the beginning.

22

The cold waves splashed against the brick castle ferociously. Winds were coming in hard, blowing to the east, towards the gates to Midghard.

Jotunheim's cold was being exchanged with warmer air. The change of climate brought questions to the Giants minds. They depended on the winter, born by it, and lived by it. Now that it was depleting, the topic of Ragnarok was now brought back to life.

Inga was curled next to a brimstone chimney that sparked with a young fire. She watched the smoke drift up into its chimney. She was contemplative of what to do next, and where to go, for she knew time wasn't on her side, nor her own will.

The Giants talked among themselves on a giant table, drinking and eating above her, the talks of the end times made her shiver. She couldn't fathom any of the concerns that floated around the room.

Ratatoskr was climbing the rafters of the tall hall of the castle, he was looking for food and something to occupy his busy mind.

He watched the giants eat the fish they had just caught when they first met on the docks. Delicious, gigantic fish — not for a squirrels mouth, but only a Giants. He saw the cups of ale sitting in front of them, big enough for himself to drown in, brazened by copper drawn out of the caves of the land.

"A magic boat, winds moving east, humans, such oddity," Gryolm said lighting a long wooden pipe filled with herbs, "Little Girl, why are you even here?"

"I really don't know. The boat brought us here," Inga said.

The Giant who sat across Gryolm looked unappeased by what she had said, he let out a big belch. He sat up and walked over to her, the wooden boards of the floor shaking. He looked down unto her with a beard made of ice.

"Little girl, we have not ever seen a human before, nor that gossiping squirrel," said the tall Giant known as Icsir.

"The lands are diminishing, fish barely bite, the ice is melting," he looked to the sea, pausing in reflection, "Strange this happens," he looked to the sea of ice, crumbling breaking and thawing out, "And then you show up."

"I do not know what is going on. I wish I did," said Inga still sitting gazing at the fire. She hasn't felt so lost in ages. Being in an estranged world full of giants was nothing like being lost in the nearby forests of her village. She had no time to feel home sick, nor was it in her nature, she only had the present to figure out her future.

Icsir, brains of a hot tempered stone that laid in his icy skull. He was Gyrolm's good friend, comrade, fellow soldier of their division. They were soldiers, this was their keep.

A fortitude of defense that illuminated the oceans with its frosty brazier of blue at the top. The oceans stretched to the further coasts of another realm known as Hemdyr, a city of another empire full of other frost giants.

Just as humans, they divided themselves into different empires, ideas, views of their world; some with kings, some with queens, some with powerful leaders, commanders.

This band of Giants had no King or Queen to present themselves, they did that themselves as a brandish lot of mercenaries. Without a true ruler, they appointed Gyrolm as one, but received the equal treatment.

They sought out only peace and by that they knew defense from the other kingdoms would bring it. Inga didn't know of this, but Ratatoskr did, he knew of everything, the gossip, the rumors of the nine worlds, but his short term memory loss did not help the matter.

The rafters that hung the few but plenty fish to dry was boarded up above making another smaller room for the guests, Inga and the Squirrel.

They slept peacefully to the smells of the Jotunheim Sea, the salts of it helped relieve their racing minds, but it also dehydrated their tongues, but they stayed peacefully asleep. They both had a long day.

Gyrolm and Icsir retreated into the lower floors of the keep along with their soldiers, a couple stayed guard in the upper levels peering out into the seaside from a balcony of wood that held the giant figures.

There was no war, nor any worry that something would happen, but it was protocol to always be on the lookout. The land was impenetrable, it held many warriors, soldiers of the coast with villages of them stretching out. If a sound was made, whatever the sound was, it would not exist after they dealt with it.

Tonight was different for everyone. The winds blew the same chilling air from the sea, cold, frozen to the bone. Inga awoke to it. The violent creaking and shaking of the rafters sounded through the keep. She thought the whole building was going to go down. Ratatoskr still remained asleep unbothered by it. He could sleep through anything, especially a dragon's roar.

"The end of days are near," said a strange giant tucked in the corner below them. His voice bellowed matching the bustling winds. Inga peeped her left eye open to his voice at first thinking it was actually the wind, but the words that flooded out his mouth caught her attention.

"End of days?" She quietly asked. She spoke softly to a Giant that sat below, but he heard nonetheless. Her voice calming to his ears made of hard rocky crystals, shining with beads from the lanterns glow.

"The weather is changing. Giants are fighting giants," he licked his lips with his wide blue tongue readying himself for his next words, "Ragnarok be upon us. End of days. The stories that tell us of the end of the world. Even your Gods can not stop it." He climbed himself up burrowing his head into the rafters, gigantic eyes matching Inga's whole body. "You say Odin sent you by a boat, but the trickster is who really sent you."

Inga pulled herself up, her tiny figure replicating itself to the Giant's pupil. The winds churned the stone architecture, shaking it a little more. The Giant licked his cold blue lips once more to the sight of little Inga.

She couldn't think of anything more, a reason to why she ended up in Jotunheim. The stories never spoke or sung of such an instance.

"What is your name?" She asked the strange Giant who sat face to face with her. She felt the cold radiate from his flesh.

"Names do not matter in the end," the Giant said licking his giant lips. "My name is no value to you, human. All worlds will perish, mangling into one. We will be long gone after, our names as well. Only the runes will tell the future kin of our stories—a bard, a song folk. Find him and have him reveal the future. Go back to your human world now," The Old grizzled Giant was irritated by what he had stumbled upon.

Midghard was vast, especially for a child. Finding a Bard that would save the nine's ending would be a challenge. She believed the Giant though. She saw it in his shimmering eyes of ice. Her boat though, it was sunken in the depths of the voids that were known as the oceans of Jotunheim.

23

The waters were hazy, marked by the masked figure in front of him. Ahlifer was paralyzed by fear, restrained by what grabbed hold of him.

He tried snapping out of the trance he was instilled in; dwarfs, bards, the nine worlds that were being consumed to the fires and ice — the original life of this universe. He saw the blackness, the floating of ice particles meeting in the middle of the black canvas, along with specks of fire. They wrapped together like a leathered handle for a recently sharpened sword, twisted into one, a cruel tool with a dichotomy of it's other.

The vivid images passed turning into memories. The ghastly figure in front of him who mimicked him was Loki all along. He felt the water in his lungs now.

The God only wanted his mind for the time being and when he saw himself only going in circles, trying to escape his once brothers' vengeance, he knew he had to let this little boy die.

He was back underneath the water, repeating the same motions over. The God was not pleased in what he saw from the events. He saw he did make it to the places where he was hoping he'd go. Loki was hoping the Urd's would be more respectful with his choices, but they still did not play according to the fates he wanted.

"You did not listen to your king," He disappeared in a smoky silhouette that stuck to the rocks below the waters. Ahlifer was still latched to now a real chain that dug into the sand beneath.

He kicked, screamed with bubbles replacing his voice, feeling that it was now all too real — he was dying and was meant to die; the memories of dwarves, his sister, the squirrel, his father and his friends… they were memories that never were to be, but only an empty map.

Inga dove into the ocean to her brother. She swam to him, grabbing his arm bringing up. This time no chain was there to hold him. He was light like a pellet that sunk instead of skipped, left to be missed.

She held her brother in her arms with tears pouring down her face matching the rain that fell from the sky. Purple and blue, Ahlifer laid still. She wanted to see him get up. She never saw him so quiet it made her even more upset.

"What happened?" Fjorn ran down to her, axe in hand in preparation for whatever made his daughter scream so loud. It wasn't anything that would draw blood — the silence could never be maimed. He saw Inga hold Ahlifer in her arms. He dropped the axe to his side immediately running towards him, eyes turning red.

He wrapped his arms around his dead son. Holding him as if it was the first day he was brought into this life. He swore to himself over and over. Inga on his side crying quietly, she trying to hold back the pain that wasn't going away.

"What happened? What happened, Inga?" His eyes stayed on his son just in case he woke. "I can not take anymore loss. I can not do it," he continued to beckon to the Gods while looking up into the starry sky hoping for an answer.

"He slipped in with the fish. He never came back up," Inga said still eyes fixed below the water. She knew her brother was a good swimmer. She wished she pulled him up.

Regrets filled her head. The things of the past that she could have done, said to avoid this situation. She bursted into more sobbing again.

Later into the later hours Fjorn sat silent in a corner outside of the room where his son laid dead. He drank his mead, his ale. He ate his musty bread and the sweet elk jerky. He was in solace when alone. His thoughts were closer to him than any man could be. But like any mortal man, those thoughts could also act against him. He drank more.

Drank more after more. He put himself in a drunken coma, head lying on the wooden table. Sleeping still, peacefully while drenched in his own piss.

He dreamt of the times his loved ones were alive. Of the times where life was a gift rather than a curse. He saw his wife in his dreams.

He touched her long amber hair once more. He saw Ahlifer reunited with her. Everyone was happy once more. Where the unending feelings of bliss, happiness were continuous with no interruptions of the pain.

He

hugged his wife once more, kissing her on her silent lips. He missed them — the feeling he got when his lips touched hers. When he caressed her body to his. He missed…her. Now he misses his son. He missed everyone he failed to protect.

A loud thud of the wooden door slammed shut after being whipped open. Fjorn sprung his head up groaning from the still drunken, impending hangover he was feeling. It was still dark out, the rain was still going. He looked around the room for who slammed the door. He thought it must have been the wind, so he laid his throbbing head down once more.

"Only the fool consumes more drink than he must," said a strange voice. It was directed at Fjorn. It was right behind him. The room was too dizzy for him to look more for the body of the voice. "How do you protect your loved ones when you are this drunken? Can you hold an axe right now?" The voice again stubbornly mocking him.

Fjorn could not push any words out his lungs besides a grumble. In his head he wanted to know who the stranger was, but the mead in his belly would only tell the man something else. The man dressed in a long leather coat and a beard to match peered into the open dim lit area in the next room.

"You lose a son, now you have none. Now you are vulnerable to your own remaining wits. Yet they play against you like the nemesis that was sworn to you from birth," continued the strange man now sitting next to Fjorn. He took his hat off, putting it on the table in front of Fjorn's groggy head. He brushed his hair back holding his gnomic words back.

Fjorn was in no mood for a fight, nor could he in his health at that moment. He slid off his chair falling to his knees on the side of his chair. Spilling spoons and forks to the side. He was weak in this state and the Stranger knew it and that is why he came.

The Stranger picked him up from the ground setting him up like a doll that tipped over. He felt pity for the man. For he should, for he was the Father of all.

He pulled his long hair back from his face showing the one eye that remained to Fjorn — hoping to spread the fear that would sober him up.

Fjorn tried standing up, clumsily holding onto the nearby table. His own grace only showed insolence. The

God saw him spin in his own head while trying to regain the balance of the world.

"You are Odin," Fjorn spun a little more falling back to his knees.

"If I was Odin, what words would you speak to me right now?" The God said quickly back. He slapped the half full mead onto the ground next to Fjorn to show his displeasure.

"I'd ask if I could see my boy again, my wife, my loved ones," tears trickled down Fjorn's bright red drunken cheeks. He started to remember his dream again—how close he was to them and yet so far. Different realms. Different worlds. Yet, they still resided in his mind.

Odin picked the drunk up from his knees, setting him face to face to him. He slapped his right cheek making sure the burn inside his nerves would be a more sobering threat than his missing eye would be, but Fjorn still dwelled in his self pity.

Odin reached in his leather knapsack—handcrafted and gifted by the Ivaldi Brother's themselves. A special reminder of times that were also broken by Loki. Now, the bag still remained inclusively for these times when the Trickster's jokes went too far.

"You are going to see what the Aesir see. You will never be drowned in the sorrows of mortality," Odin went on giving more confusion to Fjorn's already mumbled head, "you will be able to see farther than the world's have to offer. You are the Vitki that remained silent. Now, remember." With that, Odin spit in his hands with dust he gathered from his knapsack and rubbed them in Fjorn's own eyes.

He watched the mortal man scream in agony as if a hundred arrows pierced his torso. He watched him curl into a ball pissing himself from the fear he saw. He watched the blood seep out of his mortal sockets. He stood back as it all unfurled. He then saw Fjorn stand up shaking, sober, with thoughts that resigned his own.

"What is this? Fire, water, ash?" Fjorn stood up looking into the rafters of the old wood lodge. He saw into his own mind and not the world around him. He saw mountains brimmed with ash and cinder. Gods all on golden seats weapons in hand while they awaited their actions— their actions that would halt the world's end.

"The world's ending. The final chapter of these nine world's. You see it with the ashes of the nine world's stars," Odin went into his bag again gathering roots, "This is Yggdrasil's root, part of it, it will stop the hurt from what you see." He put it into his own mortar and smashed it with a hand carved hammer. Green fumes dispersed with each stroke climbing the air, sticking to the wood above.

Odin sniffed the air. It was ready. He slowly breathed it in, nostrils inflamed by the noxious sweet gas that filled the air around him. His cheeks filled like an elven balloon, he let the green air back out into the eyes of Fjorn's.

Fjorn rubbed his eyes until Odin pulled them away, "Let it sting, let it burn, let it hurt. This is the world you now see." He watched the mortal man see into the world not from a mortal's eye, but the Gods'. An unwritten prophecy, an unsung song, an unmarked stone, a rune that never touched the magics of the nine, an unwanted Vitki now born from the natures of the nine.

Fjorn would now play as an ally against the end of the worlds.

Better ask for too little than offer too much,
Like the gift should be the boon;
Better not to send than to overspend.

-Hávamál

<u>24</u>

Another day passed by, another night, another hour without her brother. Inga sat next to the bed where her brother used to lay. Now burnt to ash on a pyre made of wood and other sacrifices; meat, swords, axes, many things to offer to the Gods for an easy path to the afterlife for their beloved Ahlifer.

She could not leave the room. Her eyes stayed somberly affixed to the empty bed. Tears pulled her into deep thoughts — regrets, past mistakes, and the "what ifs" that would have kept her brother alive. She shouldn't have let him swim, it was a jest, a joke.

She knew her brother was always stuck in his head and his spirit was none of a warrior, she wanted that so she always made him do things he was not comfortable with.

Out in the other room was quiet, her father was gone now. She figured it was a drunken walk through their village. He needed his mind straight, she knew that. She did not like to see him drink when sad.

He wanted the pain away every time it hurt, he drank and drank always believing it would go away, but it still remained now with a different pain. She hated it, but she did not say anything, it would only make her do things she would regret.

She was not ready for desperate actions, she knew where it would lead, so she stayed in silence still eyeing down the bed. They burned Ahlifer like they burned everyone else in the village, in fear of the dead not liking their own deaths. Draugr, men and women who did not die a warrior's death and succumbed to the magics of Hel.

Where they would mindlessly fight until worthy of Valhalla and if defeated again, they would die and die and die all over again and again and again.

"Ahlifer, if you can hear me. Listen," she licked her lips that were salted with her own tears, "Listen once more, brother. I did not mean to make this happen. I do not know why the Gods summoned you now, especially through drowning. I hate them now. I will make this right," she crackled, tears now streaming down her face. "I will make this right. Wait for me, Brother. Wait. I will bring you back."

Face cold as ice, bony like a giants', and tired like the draugr who did not rest. Ullfr was not much of a talker, nor did he ever appreciate when spoken to. He would say what he wanted to say and expected no reply. He was the Jarl and by that title he wanted respect. He was known to be The Mad. He never slept, nor could he. He showed up in the village like a ghost preparing a haunt; quietly, sneakily and unexpectedly strolling into town unnoticed.

He opened the door into the room where Inga sat. He closed it behind him. His lips dark blue from the spring's evening freeze. He sat down right away in a chair in the corner of the room where Inga's back sat to him.

"Girl, your brother is no more. Why do you cry?" His face cold just as his spirit. "What is ahead of us now is nothing but more desolation."

Inga raised her head to stare above the bed to see

her brother's remaining belongings sat; his shoes, tunic, and his hunting knife. All still damp and cold from the water. She was reminded of the past once more. She wanted the Jarl to stop talking about it like that. So cold and straightforward.   "Go outside for once, little one. Remind yourself why you are still here. Remind yourself of the spring's rain, the life of trees, all of that," he licked his cold lips once more, "remind yourself how weak you are not like your brother."

Inga's heart started pounding. The words her Jarl just spoke started her fury. He may be her Jarl but he was not her Father nor family. Why was he here in the first place? She wondered to herself. She cursed him for it.

"Open the gift the Gods have given you. To be alive," he continued. She was growing angrier every word he spoke, "To be alive is a gift," she could have sworn he was smiling through this.

Mocking her brother. The dead who could not defend themselves was dishonorable. "Be alive like your brother can not be." Her heart thumped like a Skald's drum, a war drum, a drum with heavy echoes that beat inside of a deserted cave. She could not feel anything anymore.

"My brother is no coward," she held her temper back. She was angry. The Jarl was pushing her to the brink and he knew that. "He is no coward, was no coward," she kept saying, now looking at him. He was in fact smiling, grinning, broken teeth showing.

The dead walk, they sometimes talk, only if they want something. The Jarl was killed in his home years ago. Knife in the back of his neck, left to die.

No one knew this besides himself and the perpetrator who did it. No names were given, but he was assumed alive until she saw the ghastly icy ghost behind her.

"You are dead," she said silently sensing the lack of heart beat he held. She kept her temper hidden, it was a weakness to show when battle was about to ensue.

Even when talking to the dead, emotions must always stay at bay. "You are dead," she said once more. "Why are you here? What do you want?" She felt the cold winter grow inside the small room.

He stood up, creaking from the rotten bones that held him together. He slid his long dangling hair back to show her the death that wreaked his body. The ice that chilled his veins.

The breath that he did not breathe, it felt as if she bore every mark of death along with him, "Hel promised me my life again if I could kill the children of the last true Vitki. Let me slumber, child.

Inga immediately went for the hunting knife and slid it to his dry throat. She dug it in pinching through the remaining nerves and blood that he had left.

He watched his eyes glassy eyes peel back into his head. Shrouds of mist fumed the room — the blood of the draugr, a gas that sifted through the lands but stayed heavily concentrated on the dead.

She shook as she watched the man she killed turn on his back. No agony was wrought, but only peace. She felt his heart beat again. She saw the love of a mortal shine back into his eyes.

"She will find you, child. She knows where Odin is taking your father," he warned gasping. He clenched his throat to say what was really on his mind, "and thank you. I did not mean for this."

"Who killed you?"

"War will come soon," he ignored her questions, falling silently to his own fate.

Inga watched him finally leave the world. She picked up his cold hand and dragged his corpse outside immediately to set it afire in fear Hel would send him back. She did not understand what was going on now, but she sees that the Gods are in this.

Inga remembered tales her Grandfather would tell her; of the Vitki's, the skalds, the ones who kept track of the worlds. Their foretelling would guide the way of the mortals, they were the eyes of the Gods.

Although the Gods could not see the future, the Vitki's could. A magic condemned by the Aesir, but condoned by the Vanir — which were constructed by their own magic.

She watched the corpse burn. The screams of Hel rung through the woods that surrounded their tiny village.

She latched onto the corpse peeling, burning, leaving nothing but bones to show. Charred remnants of what magic dwelled in the Nine.

Her mind played back and forth of the times Ahlifer, her brother would constantly talk about these demons. Men who did not want to die, but died without reaching their own destiny.

Men usurped, killed, murdered women, children, kings, jarls in the name of greed. If caught they would too die a normal death and forever be chewed by the Dragon below the World Tree — Nidhogg, he would gnaw their bones, their flesh while the murderers and thieves cried in agony for the rest of the world.

Villagers gathered around quickly weapons in hand ready to defend themselves from the ghastly screams of the dead. They looked out and saw the draugr, their Jarl burning with fire that grew from red to blue.

The Draugr remained outside of the island, into the forests, deep in caverns, but never in villages.

Edvar drunk as usual around the time came to Inga's side. Her face not the same as the child she once was. She killed, and after the first kill for any living being, something grows.

Edvar knew the beast inside her was birthed and he out of all of the lot, knew what was next.

He didn't see the little girl he once saw days ago, he now saw a woman; young in front of a man burning, on a pyre she made herself, and a kill she done herself, the animal inside her would grow bigger.

"Inga," started Edvar setting his mead down beside her. "You feel somethin', aye?"

She just stood watching, remembering the Jarl's dead face when she jabbed the hunting knife into his throat. The happiness she felt from him. She could tell if it was his happiness, or her happiness of the kill. Emotions fought emotions that made her remain still.

"Inga," he kept trying to pry her emotionless face open, "Inga, you killed a man…"

Right there, that set her off. Those words were the key to her locked heart. *You killed a man. You killed a man. You killed. A. Man. A living being.* The words kept echoing back. She had only killed squirrels, boar, deer, rabbits, all of the like, but never a human being. Her heart dropped immediately as if those words opened the chains of emotions that held her so complacent.

Thud, thud, thud, thud went her heart. She felt the wind on her hair, the ash of the man she killed touch her skin, the happiness, the sadness, the anger. She killed a man. It finally hit her.

"Inga, shite. I ain't good at this helpin' cope shite out thing," he kept going when all she wanted was to stay to herself and think and restring her heart back to the wall she built to hide it. "You... well, I'll let you." He stopped talking, picked up his mead and stared at the glowing fire in front of him. He cursed himself. "Where the fuck is Fjorn when you need this father figure type shit?" He spat to the side.

It was too late now.

The fire had just started.

The dead are walking.

Brothers are dead.

Kin in shambles.

Inga walked away with no words, passing through the other villagers, their eyes affixed on her. A child who killed the Jarl. Many people talked amongst eachother.

"Is she the jarl now?" One chuckled among the crowd. He was half drunk, so everyone else was.

"She is a usurper!" Mumbled another.

"Finally someone killed that wretched man," yelled an old lady covered in tans, and with that, cheers sounded the area, "Heil Odin for her!" They sung, "Heil the All-Father!"

Inga ignored it all. She walked faster to the edges of the woods and into the brushes where Odin's Wolf's spirit laid. She needed answers. This would be her place of solitude where her home was now not.

<u>25</u>

Winds whispered through the woods, the leaves sputtered around loosely off the branches onto the ground. Chipmunks, birds, squirrels pattered and spoke among each other. The morning dew stuck to rocks and the air whistled when met with it.

Inga, eyes still aflame from the atrocity she had seen, the words her Father's friend, Edvar had spoke. If her father were around, he would have already started searching for her, but he was not. The dead were walking— Hel was searching for her and her family. Was it her that killed her brother? The question never disappeared after seeing the draugr speak about it.

A vitki? A seer? What was it with these legends, these fairy tales coming to life she thought? Why was she involved, why was her brother? Was her mother killed because of it? She stopped.

She could not handle anymore questions. She remembered her Father's words, *if you think more than you have to, you will have more questions than answers.*

She ducked under a broken log that perched and wedged itself into another tree. All the trees were wrapped in moss and dew, glossy and clean looking. Clean for what nature was intended to be. When humans did not touch it.

The woods felt like another world.

She thought if her Brother were still alive, he'd be dancing through the broken branches with a broken branch himself, wielded in his hand like a sword, battling invisible creatures.

She missed him. She missed everyone. She missed her youth that was butchered when she killed the Jarl. She couldn't stop thinking of past regrets.

She hated not being able to communicate with her own soul, her intuition she so needed right now. She felt weak. She just felt that if anyone would know what was going on, it were these child hood fairy tales—a last hope acted upon desperation.

She would have laughed if her Brother came up with the idea about searching Odin's Forest Wolves' out. He was always so naïve to reality, or was he? Maybe there was some truth to his imagination. She felt sad again. As soon as the emotion hit, her brother's face disappeared.

The loneliness crept on her until she heard something running up above her.

"Slow down! This is urgent," the voice squeaked. "Business from One-Eye!" It kept running above, climbing itself down from the large trees. Its breathing was rapid. Each breath trying to catch up to the other.

"A squirrel that talks?" Inga said to it, "First the dead walk in a village, now a squirrel."

"Got you to talk. Let's skip the Boar shit, cut to the chase. I'm here to," the little squirrel stopped talking still trying to catch up to its breath, "One second."

Inga still showed no sign of excitement of seeing a talking rodent. She did not care. She needed to find the Wolves. She waited for him to speak again to see what the magical rodent wanted from her, or had to say.

"Fack! I been chasin' you for miles, yard, whatever distance you guys keep," he stopped again. "We have to go, and when I say go, I mean go. We have to go to the lake. No skipping stones, jumping what be it. Orders from the All-Father," he stopped again catching the last of his breath, "Fack, thought I was going to die there. Okay, so follow me," he started hopping down the opposite path she was on.

"I'm finding the Wolves, the spirits Odin left behind here to guard Midgard," Inga said still keeping her direction, not caring where the little rodent went. "If you want to follow, so be it, but I'm going this way."

The Squirrel stopped, and immediately ran back to her, clawing her legs to turn her body to follow the direction he was going to, "No! You stubborn som'bitch, you will be following me. Odin. Fackin' Odin demands it! He says, 'find the little girl, take my boat along the path of the giants, the rivers will guide you along the branches'," he grumbled. "Now follow. Come on, girl follow me," he slapped his little leg as if she was his giant dog.

"Odin? What's he doing here? Why did he send a squirrel?" She asked kicking him away irritated by his little claws poking her leg.

"Name's Ratatoskr, the shite-talking squirrel who loves to gossip and stuff. Follow me now. Come on!" He was in a hurry. When the Head of the Aesir demanded something, it was urgent, especially with Ratatoskr. "The wolves you seek, they are just legend made by mortals. Nothing else, so you are just going in circles, now follow once more… PLEASE."

Inga shrugged at him. She had no other choice anymore, especially if this little squirrel could take her to Odin, or anything that would answer her own questions.

26

"I saw you in the boy's memories," Loki was displeased on what he saw, how the Volga had turned him down when asking for questions, "I demand answers from here on. You put me on this path, and when I saw you turn me down, I will now not walk away this time," he smirked. He pressed his finger on the tip of his knife.

Sajja and her sisters were quiet, they were too busy meditating to the forests pleas; the cries for help, the fears of something monstrous coming. "We can not tell you more, Trickster," said Sajja stopping her séance, one eye opened to him, the other in the realms of unborn nature. "We have already done a terrible act of changing the course of time by giving you up the last Vitki," she paused again, breathed in the air, the foul air. "Mortals, unlike Gods, will push back without logic — anger, violence, revenge will behold them. I can not tell you more. Now leave."

Loki quickly in a blink of an eye, swiftly like the wind flew up to her with his dagger's tip now pointed to her throat, "You will tell me more." He was angry, not with himself, no. He had an ego too big to put the guilt on him. He was too pretentious, too headstrong to admit he had caused this.

She didn't say anything back. The wise always held their tongues when arrogance was used, even when it was a God that displayed it. She continued to ignore the pleading God after that, but kept that one eye open to survey his movements.

He was panicking, walking back and forth dagger still flailing outward towards her. His eyes flaming with fire, kindled by her passiveness.

Loki remained in his own thoughts too, he tried to get back on track, to the trickster he was, the one who pried open other's own thoughts with their own integrity. He wasn't himself anymore. He was reckless. He knew that. Who was he supposed to seek guidance from if the Volga would not?

"I was selfish, I must apologize for that," he stopped collecting his own thoughts, turning them once more into his ally from the enemy they were becoming, "Where do I go from here?"

Sajja remained quiet. Eyes both closed now

focusing on the crying of the nature around her. She tried to tend it before it became too late.

She was also infuriated her own self for turning the fates. It caused the dying of the unborn below the grounds, the magics that were diminishing, and the cries of the unborn.

"I will remain quiet with you then, Witch," he hoped by calling her that, it would push something to open her up. He played with everyone, especially their weaknesses. She though remained quiet still tending to the unborn as a mother would with her crying baby.

"If you can not help me, then I have no other choice," he muttered to himself while becoming irritated once more from her silence. He turned his blade once more to her throat, her eyes both opening softly as it touched her tattooed skin. "If you are not needed by a God, you are not needed by this world," he watched her eyes close as if she was ready for the next moment. He slit her throat open watching the blood and remaining energy she once had.

"You... killed.... The worlds," she gasped letting the world take her. Her sister's screaming and fled for the tree lines. He swiftly stopping them in their own tracks with his knife to their throats.

He stopped to look at the dead Volga around him. The animals they tended were gone, the spirits gone, the magic that barred them inside their own sanctuary now depleting.

The end was coming, and he welcomed it now.

Where was he supposed to go now? He still had many Volga's that would answer him, but he took it upon himself play the All-Father. He would never be Odin, but he could be something else, something more than a god of war, a god of all wisdom, he could, and would be the end.

He knew how to read the runes, he knew how to find a way, to get his way, to find answers without meaninglessly digging through books, listening to skald's sing their own world's tales, he always had a way.

He now needed allies in this impending war that was about to come. He would not question himself on how to make them, but he questioned on whom will listen, and if not they listen, who to provoke.

He looked at his blade, still with the Volgas' blood. He smiled to himself not in self worth, but conceit, trying to turn away the self pity that would wrought from fully knowing what he was doing.

He did not know what he was doing, but he never did, he always wanted a laugh, but this joke he had started, would end in no punch line, but only hurt.

"Odin, if you hear me right now. I am turning the tides of the Gods' fates. You may be pleased, you may not. I have not the slightest on how you feel about this," he laughed to himself knowing Odin would not hear him, but hoping one of his Raven's would. They were always spying. Always following. Always gathering information of the worlds. "I will be back by supper, papa!" He mockingly laughed to the sky. No answer still. "Send a Raven here, or you may have a Raven already here, but your Volga's are dead. The Vanir will be displeased, I know of this. I am making more enemies than I should be, but I have a plan," he slid his dagger in his belt. A large thunder bolt crashed in front of him. He smiled at that.

"Oh, hello Thor!" He smiled up in the now thundering clouds. "No Odin?" He kept his eyes peeled towards one particular cloud in blue static. "Are you coming down? Or are you just going to sit on that pedestal of yours?"

A crushing roar came furrowing down into the ground in front of him. Behind it was Thor, still staticky from the lightning of the clouds. His face was stern, angered by his kin in front of him. Loki loved every second of it, he cherished it more than life to see Thor especially angry with him.

"You killed the Volga," Thor said with anger, "If Odin finds out," he was cut off by a laugh that was meant to anger him even more than he was.

"Odin will. I know. I see his Ravens fluttering about above me, but maybe you killed them with that juvenile acting out you did from the skies," he smiled, grabbing once more for his dagger. Thor quickly grabbed his wrist, twisting it. He heard the cracks of his own bones, but Loki still smiled into his kin's eyes. "I know you won't kill me."

"Don't be certain, Fool. Odin wants you dead as

well. Along with Tyr, and the others. Even the Vanir will now since you killed their own," Thor spoke of the Volga, they were a gift to the Aesir from the Vanir when their feuds ended. Odin wanted wisdom, more than his Raven's could give him when he wasn't in the other worlds, so he asked for the Volga's.

Loki twisted his wrist out, releasing it from Thor's grasp. He licked his lips and waved his hands in the air showing he will further remain unarmed.

"You will come back to Asgard to face your trial. This ends now," Thor slid Mjolnir out of his latch and pointed the blunted end to Loki's chin. The runes on his turned to bright yellow matching the thunder that struck in Thor's own eyes.

"I am sorry but I have other plans right now," Loki pushed the hammer away from his face. "Care to join? Or you too busy being your Father's errand boy?" He smirked.

Thor waved his hammer towards Loki's right cheek, but he was too quick to take the blow. He had other plans to be pummeled down by Thor and Mjolnir. In truth he had no idea what he was doing, but he was Loki, and knowing that, the plans would arise when they were meant to.

"Goodbye, Thor," he smiled at the Aesir, now yards away from him. Thor eyed him down with anger and rage as he vanished into the mists of the woods that surrounded him.

Thor stood still in the woods, now drenched with the rains that he conjured from his storms, his Mjolnir in his right hand and the left tending his wet beard. He has always hated Loki.

For many reasons. He had gone farther this time, he usually could brush it off, but this time he could not. He took in all the memories where Loki had entangled him in his own charades — one being when he cut the roots of his wife's beautiful blonde hair, it made her devastated, depressed, weak.

He was the one who had to be there for her, while Loki would be trodding along all merrily trying to fix the problem he created. It usually ended up good, but this time Thor feared it would not. This time he saw Loki would bring everyone down with him.

Asgard was the home of the Aesir, a tribe that consisted of Warriors, immortal and fearful, yet well deserving of praise. Thor would refuge here, he would seek council from the others for the next move. He had found Loki, but he disappeared too quickly to catch.

Tyr was in front of the half-built wall a giant who tricked them had started. He knew nothing good was going to come to the actions of his kin. He wanted to prepare for the worse.

He always stayed defensive expecting war of any nature to break out. He had to. It was why he was there.

"Almost had him," Thor said walking through the light snow towards Tyr. "I had him and he wiggled his way out like the snake he is," Thor admired the snow, the cold on his skin, but wondered why it was there near the bridge to Jotunheim. "Why is it colder over here?"

Tyr unlatched his cloak of silver fabric lying it down on the ground neatly. He picked up a clump of the snow and clenched it in his hand. His face was dark, Thor did not like what he saw from his expression, he had other plans, and it was not to fight his way out, but to deceive his way out.

"It became colder, snow started falling from the branches held high," Tyr dropped the remaining snow from his hand on to the ground, watching it fall gracefully, "You remember the stories? Yes?" He looked at Thor with darkness, "War, the end, all of it."

"Ragnarok," Thor finished for him, "I know. Odin told me when I was young. This is why the snake needs to be caught. I am not taking it lightly if that's what you're trying to say," he thought of the snow and how light it was, the circumstances of it, and why it was falling. He remembered the more of the stories and the second phase of Ragnarok, *Fimbulwinter*.

"We need this wall finished," Tyr touched the side of the huge unfinished wall cutting to the point. He glanced along the cracks seeing the loose stone on the side that was to be finished. "The Giant did this on purpose. We cannot trust anyone anymore besides ourselves."

"We can trust the mortals."

"We can if you think it is wise," Tyr immediately said looking back at Thor, face still dark. "Why though?

Friends can become enemies if you give them more trust than they deserve, brother."

The Thunder God didn't think like Tyr and that was why in this time it was important to have him on their side. With no Baldr, who could fix it all, they had to resort to the rest of the Aesir and use their strengths to maintain their game plan. They needed to live.

"Where are your sons?" Tyr did not hesitate to keep asking him questions.

"Vanaheim, I assume. I sent them there to deliver the message of Loki's whereabouts and to announce the deaths of their own Volga's."

"Our," Tyr frowned, "We are in this together. Our gifts are the Vanir's as well, even if given to us, we are together. The rest of the nine may not, but we still have Vanaheim."

Thor looked to the sky, the sun, *Sol*, coming down to the edge for a night's rest, awaiting for its sister, *Mani*, the moon to come out to play. He pictured the two siblings now being swallowed by the children of the Fenris Wolf, *Fenrir*. Loki's son. The world's destruction would be Loki's doings, and the sons and daughters of him as well.

"The father's sins will forever stain this world," Thor said aloud still imagining the desolation of it, "We need to find this damned Wolf. I believe that should be our next plan." He was getting ahead of himself. He was talking over Thor from his own fears.

"Yes, we do. First, the wall. The Giants will break through, their armies will take over. We have to defend this," Tyr talked as if it could be any time soon. Any moment, but not out of fear, but out of discipline and the structure of keeping Asgard safe. He knew this time it wouldn't be only a hundred giants, but thousands upon thousands. Time was their only friend at the moment.

"Where is Odin?" Asked Thor taking in mind of what his fellow Aesir has said, "He needs to know of these plans."

"He found the Vitki, the mortal of Vanir blood, he is with him. Loki had killed the son. Used him for his memories. But we have the father of him," Tyr looked up into the sky again, stoic and tall, his golden armor shined and speckled to the sun's ending light. "He will know. The Ravens are telling him everything as we speak."

27

Odin let Hugin, his Raven flutter back into the night sky. The news of the nine worlds was received. Now it was time for him to come up with his own plan of action.

Odin had all the wisdom any mortal would have wanted thanks to the Vanir, Mimir, and the Ravens, and Volga's. The problem was that Loki used that to his own advantage.

"My Volga's of Midgard are dead," Odin frowned while brushing his hands on his long coat, "We will finish this now."

Fjorn was trudging through the dense forest blindingly. His eyes were scarred from the flames and magic Odin conjured upon them.

His throat hoarse from the screaming. He tried to talk as much as he could, but words barely would seep through his lips. He remained quiet though, most of the journey taking in the sounds of the unfamiliar animals that talked.

He heard everything; the dying of plants, fauna, animals, and even the births of which. He heard the life and death that surrounded him. He still could not see anything else.

His eyes pulsed to every motion. Every tree branch or inanimate object he walked by, he felt the runes pulse through the world he was in. Legs sore from the walking were now ignored by it all. He felt the wind bellow and talk to him, words he could not understand, but he knew they were informing him of something. Everything was more alive, also deader…

"Where are you taking me?" Asked Fjorn in a cold voice, crackled by a broken speech.

"The tree I hung from for three days," Odin spoke confidently, "You will hang for three days, you will not die if that's how you see fit for your life."

Fjorn thought of Ahlifer's life. He wondered if the last thought his boy was *I want to die*. His boy was not strong in physicality, but his head was. He couldn't imagine it anymore. His death. It hurt his eyes even more. The burning would go on when he done so. So he stopped.

"My boy, where is he? Did he want to die? Why is this different?" Fjorn hurt when he spoke, his voice like a dagger in his own throat, such as the one that killed his boy.

His mind played against him.

"I do not know. You will find him though. Just stay on this path, it is your path," Odin stopped in his tracks to look at the tree once more. He fell silent. He remembered the pain, he remembered wanting to die and to let go, but the thirst for knowledge and answers kept him alive. "This is it. This is where your journey starts, my friend," Odin's voice picked back up again.

"Starts?" Fjorn could barely say the word. He could not think of the journey before, the loss he endured, was that not the start already? "My journey started from when I lost my loved ones," he forced the words out with anger.

"We are always changing, and yes we Gods are as well. Nothing is complete until our fates are aligned once more," the gnomic words confused Fjorn, but he remained silent listening to the God he had praised all his life, "You are of Vanir blood. Your family. You will always experience something more.

You can drink your sorrows away, but what good does that do? It only stopped the process of making more memories, making the wisdom Men and Gods' alike thirst for. You right now are too weak, Fjorn," Odin's words hit Fjorn like a rusted arrow, spitted with venom straight into his chest, "and now your pride is damaged. Good, now you know what it's like to becoming a true God."

Odin picked the man up from his legs, and gently wrapped the noose around his throat. He saw the air leave his body, seeing his eyes combust with flames again. He saw the mortal man struggle from instinct. He felt pity for him, but only because he was hanging his own creation.

"You will not die, Fjorn. Know. Know that you will survive. Know that tomorrow will come. Know that I will be back in three days," Odin let him drop, he watched the man kick from the sudden stoppage of breath that was supposed to come after the next. It was too tight, it cut off his voice allowing him to be only speak with his thoughts. He was now with himself only, and the nature that bended around him.

The tree would be either his grave or his redemption, "Learn what it is like to die. It will help you find out what it is like to die. Death is only an answer within an answer, I speak only with wisdom, Fjorn."

With that he left the undying man who kicked and thrashed from the death that would not come. He hoped he would find the ally the man needed; his thoughts, his conscious, his own insight, and not the mortal remedies. He wanted him to lose all of it.

He wanted him to find the wisdom the old oak would give him. In mean time, he had to go Muspelheim, to try and make a deal with the Fire Giant, Surtr.

He saw the memories, was told of them by his Raven's, they saw it for themselves, how Loki killed the boy, how he murdered the Volga's of the Vanir, how he consecrated the Gifts of the world for his own misdeeds.

In Muspelheim, the ground was lava, the trees were charred, but still remained. Surtr made sure of it, to keep the lands ablaze for his own comfort. He was created when Fire and Ice converged long long ago. When Ginnungagap only existed, it eventually separated into two, Muspelheim and Niflheim were the new worlds, when fire and ice clashed, and they were always separated. The balance.   Surtr sat on a giant fiery steed.

His sword, Solvangr, always alit with the flames from his lands. Forever brimming with ash and steel. The world was bright, dark, but still bright from the blistering heat. All creatures were made of fire and soil. Giants of Fire, all of them, burning with fiery axes and swords, mail, and plate, with steeds of their own.

Odin always hated the sites of the first worlds. It always made him remember his own father, Ymir, a Giant of Frost. One of the reasons why he never came back is that they both share an enemy, and that is of the Fire Giants. He stayed Ymir ages ago, he hated how cruel he was to creation. Used them only for his own and did not give them freedoms they deserved from birth.

The All-Father walked, thundering down the long bridge where at the end he would face Surtr. He has long spoke to him since his Father's surmising death. The Fire Giant bared to attention to the Aesir as he walked down the bridge of coal and embers.

Two dogs barked, their growls led streams steam out of their illusive mouths.

"Who comes?" Said Surtr with a huge growl that made all volcanoes boil. They surrounded all the landscapes, made up all the oceans in Muspelheim.

"Fire Giant! What do you want with the Vitki?" He sneered seeing Surtr turn to him. His eyes were no eyes but two gems that burned to his unrelenting rage. "I hear you want him."

"Want a man? Some mortal? Why would you assume that?"

"I do not know, but your magic was involved in a memory I have received from Mimir," Odin coughed to the dryness that was caused from the land. His spat at the lake of lava on the side of the bridge he was on, "His eyes burned with your magic. Pure fire. Tell me, did Loki come to you? And if he did, you must tell me," Odin was infuriated. His anger was blinding him. He had both of his sons killed in front of him, one by him, and one by Loki, but in the end, they were both by the Trickster.

"Your emotions are strong, Aesir!" Surtr said back at him while his hounds still barked viciously at the Old God. "This isn't like you. Where is that wisdom that burns? It's all rage now." Surtr mocked him, but also was genuinely concerned — not for the Aesir, but of the World's above. "Loki has never been here, nor have I seen him in ages. He is no Giant. He is only for himself."

Odin finally made it to Surtr himself. His eyes sweaty, and glossy from the heat that burned to the core. His skin boiling, and his missing eye aflame from the patch that held over it. The weather would kill Odin, but it would not stop him from getting answers.

"Explain the Gebo that branded his chest. What gift were you to give him?" Odin was trying to get answers, but the Fire Giant had no idea what he was asking. Surtr never had access to the runes as is, but the magic that burned in the memory of Fjorn branded by the "X" Gebo, was a magic that came right from Muspelheim.

"Aesir!" Shouted Surtr, volcanoes now roaring, his steed now neighing heavily and thunderously, "You do not come to my realm and threaten me! The Fire Giants had nothing to do with this, nor did I."

Odin snorted, wiping his lips from the sweat that drenched him, holding his arms of the boils that were about to pop and kill him, "Magic. Who knows it here?" He cut right to the chase. The heat would kill him at any time and he needed answers quickly. "Give me a Volva of your land. I will bring her back when done." One of them would know, and that's why he needed her. If Surtr did not know of what was going on under his rank, the seeress would. They would not speak of the end, but they would hint it for him, and they would also know more of the magics.

"I can not," rattled Surtr, "Return to your sky."

"Now!" Bellowed Odin. The fiery skies turned to rain. It dripped and steamed from the heat, "If you want your world to live another day, for you to live another day, give me a Volva, I will return her," he held tightly on his wounded arms, "Or drown in the rain that will come," he looked up into the thunderous sky at his son, Thor creating them, hands out while his chariot led by his goats,

Tanngnjóstr and Tanngrisnir stayed on the paths. In an out of fiery clouds, turning them into dust while the chariot zig-zagged in between them.

Surtr eyed the Thunder God high above. His eyes staying focused on the golden chariot, he two goats that ran through the winds. He was displeased of the two Aesir coming to his lands and causing such troubles. He wanted to kill them both for it, but he knew that would only start a war he could not win. He turned back to Odin with displeasure and pain that came from the tiny water droplets that seared his skin, "You can have the Volga for now, I will send her tonight."   "

No tricks, Surtr," barked Odin back, now with his skin searing with steam from the rain.

"No tricks," Surtr was lacking his complacent confidence he once bore before. He thought he had the Aesir in the corner of not giving him what he demanded. He cared more for his World, he would not let it be turned into another Niflheim; a misty, dense, freezing wasteland. He did this for himself, he reminded himself of that when the two Aesir had their leave.

"She will return in two cycles!" Odin now showing of his good intentions. He was too weak to argue back and forth due to the land's terrible weathers. He knew Thor would not be able to soak the world dry, but Surtr on the other hand, did not, and that is why he used that to his advantage, to break the Fire Giant's confidence and turn it into fear.

28

It was dark now, the moon had set its course to only grow higher through the midnight sky. The trees now covered in the fog that stood above the branches, glistening like torches held high. Inga and Ratatoskr were closer to the boat, according to the squirrel they were.

In fact, he had not the slightest clue on where to go, but it was a boat to Jotunheim. How? Through a magic portal, the rickety wooden boat would sail them through the branches of Yggdrasil, the dew that stuck to them would be their river.

It was quiet, no animals made a sound, only the grumbling of the Squirrel's little belly. He hadn't eaten the whole day, he was too busy running errands for Odin, it upset him, but he wanted to be competent. He wanted to be respected among the Gods more.

He didn't want to be the little shit talking squirrel he was known for, he wanted to be the Squirrel the Gods could go to for wisdom, kind of like Odin's raven's, Hugin and Munin, like the Volga's, like someone who mattered.

It was too dark for him to see, or for Inga to know her own course. She could not hop along like a little rodent with fragile, yet versatile limbs, she felt everything; the rocks she stubbed her toes on, the branches that smacked her face, and the thorns that broke through her clothes. She still pressed on.

A talking squirrel was all she had to go on for finding out her own answers.

"Right through here," said Ratatoskr hopping through some bushes, still unclear on where he actually was going. He just felt the adventure push his own adrenaline. Inga pushed herself through the bristles of more thorns that stung her, she was bleeding from cuts where there was no clothing to protect her.

She smelt burning, wood burning, chimes that dinged together when the wind pushed through. She thought it was a good sign, until she first hand saw the three dead Volga's lying there, blood dried to their throats. "Whoa," Ratatoskr ran up to one of the dead sisters picking her arm up, "They are dead." That was a given, but Ratatoskr was known to state the obvious until it was stuck in the other's mind. "Yep, dead, fookin' dead." He dropped the arm down to the ground now sniffing the dead sisters' neck.

She ignored his actions the entire time. What caught her attention the most was the trail of blood that led outside the edges of the little grove. The tracks instantly disappeared on a line of blue dust. Some sort of magic that looked as if it dissipated.

"DO NOT TOUCH THAT!" Loudly squeaked Ratatoskr while running furiously to her side, "That's Vanir magic! Once used, and broken, it burns like a son of a bitch," he pulled her leg back with his claws, "I once seen a man touch used magic once. Lost his entire legs. Tripped right o'er a rock, landed right into it, balls and everything gone," he threw his hands up in there, "Whoosh, all gone."
She kept her distance, but it still fascinated her.

Magic in Midgard? This close to her home? She remembered tales of never venturing out into these woods. How no one ever made it alive back. She always thought it had something to do with the Wolf Spirit that lived out there. How he was the one who chewed on the bones and flesh of people with questions that would never suffice him.

They both felt the urge to look into the tents, covered in moss and some sort of animal skin both could not recognize. Skin of blue, most likely dyed from their own magics.

Ratatoskr went into one, while Inga went into another one, a much taller, wider tent. Ornaments of bones, skins of animals, and trinkets sprung through. She saw one trinket that seemed to catch her attention, a rune still glowing. She picked it up carefully without hesitation. "What do you seek here, Girl?" A Woman's voice asked. Inga jumped, she felt it breathe down her neck, the tiny hairs sticking right up. She quickly turned around hoping to see where the voice came from. Nothing. Nothing was behind her, no one.

She walked towards the exit thinking the Woman would be outside, but again, nothing or no one would be. "Your instincts seem to see what exists, but do you really trust them?" Again the Woman's voice. "Go back to that rune and tell me what it says." Again giving Inga more of a displeasing feeling.

She did what the voice said and walked toward the rune, ignoring the sounds of Ratatoskr inside the other tent — the clashes of plates and plinking of steel. She touched the rune once more, now holding it closer to her, the auras of magic burning her eyes. It hurt, but she felt it was necessary. She knew pain would always lead closer to the truth, an answer. Right now, she had no other option.

"What does it say?" The voice again now even closer as if it grew inside her head.

"I don't know," muttered Inga anxiously with her eyes still growing on the rune, "Do you know?" She asked the Woman, hoping she could tell her.

"I do."

"Tell me then."

"You tell me," The voice echoed back, "You know what it says."

"I don't though," said Inga, tears flowing from her eyes from the strange emotions she naturally conjured. She could not comprehend any of it. The voice and where it came from. The memories came flowing into her. Memories she never had before. Adventures she had never been on.

Caves with Ice Giants in Jotunheim. Ratatoskr was right there with her. Tall castles made of bricks, handcrafted by the Giants who dwelled there. She knew they were, but how?

"You now see it. You see of what could have been," said the Woman's voice. "You see how time intersects itself with its own self." The more the voice went on, the dizzier Inga became, the more uneasy she became. She did not know what was going on and the Voice only spoke in riddles and it upset her even more. She saw more and more as the voice pressed on, "You know how to read it, don't you?" Almost mocking her, "Remember what it is. REMEMBER!" Images of her brother, Ahlifer. Black figure in front of him, letting him go from his death, but bringing him back to him. Image after image. Brother now dead. Knife to throat. She screamed.

"It's the Gebo. Branded as a gift," said the voice, "A gift on how the world could turn out. I am dead because of it," the voice sounding sadder, "My sister's suffered from my own sins."

"What sins? What gift?" Inga could not understand nor fathom any of it, she was sobbing, caught in tears that flowed down her eyes and onto her lips, "I don't know the meaning of this rune."

"It's a gift I gave to Loki," the words startled Inga when she heard the Woman's voice say it, "He misused my council, my knowledge, and now wants the blood of everything your Mother touched."

Inga had no recollection of her Mother, nor who was she, all she knew of the nose, the stubby nose she had from her. How Ahlifer's mind raced, imagined the vivid images of the nine, how he thought he could see the world in it.

"Am I a God? A Vanir?" Inga wondered aloud. Was she all this time something she was not? It made her quickly question her own existences, the images that surrounded her head when holding the rune close to her.

"No," the voice responded back. "No you are not," the winds replied for her, the roaring streams winding through the tent's canopy, digging itself up.

Inga felt disappointed, if anything had turned up good on her journey, it'd be finding out she was a God. The main issue was if she could even trust this murdered soul. Was she led astray from Loki?

Inga heard Ratatoskr run, bellowing through the tent's flaps, he had treasures stacked upon his back tightly by twine and bristle. He was startled by the ferocious winds, while Inga stood silently still looking at the rune while waiting for a reply from the dead Volga.

"Wherever you go now, you must never turn your back on fate. Every road will turn you, sometimes mad, sometimes angered, sometimes it will give you a rewarding pleasure, but do not focus on those emotions, just keep going," the voice's tone turned sad, "You will find your brother, and you will find him. Listen to the trees when lost, call on the birds when in question, keep going," she paused momentarily to the winds, awaiting for them to settle a bit more, they were speaking to her still, "And if you see Loki, tell him I am sorry."

Inga did not know what she meant. She just continued her path with the wind. Trudging through the thick mud with her squirrel companion.

He swore every chance he got, picking himself through the mud with a tiny branch. A couple of acorns slung behind back with a tiny rope.

Together they would have to keep going, together they would have to go wherever the nature around them told them to go. As long as they had it on their side, they would find where they needed to be.

<u>29</u>

Thunderous roars, thrashing of chains, Sindri and Brokk
hammered the heavy nails into the ground. Tyr tied tight the
heavy cuffs around the Giant Wolf's legs. They hurried
quickly, tying him up, two other dwarves stood on heavy
platforms high above the rest, yanking a metal clasp that
rested in the Wolf's mouth so he did not attempt to kill them
all.

Sindri ran away quickly when his job was done,
backing up wiping his hands from the heavy saliva that
dripped on him. He looked up to the Giant Wolf, staring into
it's dark black eyes; ominously bright, vicious, and hungry.

Brokk did the same, quickly stepping aside to the
ale he left on a table away from the Wolf. He chugged the
whole thing down in content of his job well done.

"Why are we doing this again?" Sindri looked at his brother. He was still shaking from the adrenaline of it all. He had never seen a wolf so big, so terrifying.

"A request from the Aesir, I guess," Brokk wiped the froth from his upper lip, trying to catch his breath, "Apparently this is Loki's son."

Sindri's eyes opened wide, he could not believe what he saw, or how the two were related. He looked at the Wolf, his eyes still stinging with that same ominous glow at him, then towards Tyr who fearlessly stood in front of the Giant Fenrir, chains in hand commanding the wolf to stare into his eyes.

"Look at me!" Howled Tyr, yanking the chains of the metal clasps that sunk into Fenrir's lower jaw, bringing his face closer to him, "Trust me!" He yanked again, but the Wolf kept his eyes on Sindri. He knew it was his craft of runic metals that bound him.

Sindri felt uneasy about that, he grabbed his own ale, drinking the whole thing in one gulp, throwing it to the side of him. He felt the warmth of it hit his belly, "Why is he still staring at me?" He chewed on his finger nails nervously, simultaneously grabbing more ale from a little barrel.

Brokk did not say anything, but kept his eyes on the Aesir with the chains. He watched Tyr yank and yank on the metal chains. The Wolf still not obeying.

"Listen, Son of Loki!" Tyr said, seeing the huge eyes of the Wolf look down on him, settling himself down, "Trust me!"

Fenrir stood tall, feral hair, salivating down the chains that stuck in his lower jaw. He relaxed himself still eyeing down the God who chained him.

Tyr let the chains drop, showing his own trust. He pet the wolf's lower jaw, removing the clasps from them with the other. They dropped heavily before his own feet.

Sindri and Brokk looked at one another in awe and disbelief of what they were seeing. Tyr and Fenrir stared each other down, both dominant, confident in their own actions. The two dwarves drank to that, but mostly drank to settle their own unending nerves.

"I am honorable. I do not slay anything that is chained up," said Tyr still showing his relentless attitude towards the Wolf.

Tyr felt the salivating Wolf's jaw. He let the Wolf open its mouth. Heavy panting, and a vile stench came pouring out the Wolf's mouth.

He looked into the long wide throat of Fenrir's, sliding his arm into the back of it, showing that he did not fear him, "If you trust me, you will not…" before he could finish his words, the Wolf clenched the Aesir's arm down, crushing his armor, to skin, dripping the blood into the bone, cracking the fragments of his arm.

Tyr kept his dominance; he did not scream, did not cry, did not tear up from the pain he was feeling. Instead he pet the wolf's nose, "So you do not trust me, that is your decision."

The Wolf pulled back, ripping Tyr's arm off, swallowing it whole, still looking ominously at the God in front of him.

Tyr held his maimed arm, holding it back from the blood that poured out, he kept his word, he did not kill him right there.

He watched him chew, on the remaining ligaments of his arm. He knew that would have happened. Clenching his arm still he walked back to the two shaking dwarves in a calm manner, while Fenrir howled viciously at the moon.

"We are done here," Tyr said, bandaging up his maimed stub, "Make me an arm. Metals like the chains that hold down that fucking wolf," he took a swig of his own drink, and pouring the rest of it on his bandaged limb.

The two dwarves scuttled up the high stairs, back into the halls of Asgard. Returning themselves to their own shop.

They spent the rest of the night hammering away, clinking metals together, branding runes onto the newly done arm; the Tiwaz glew brightly on them, a mark of Tyr's own fortitude.

They drank the night away with ease they were no longer by the best, Sindri especially. His nose still tainted with the canine's foul breath.

180

That night marked the abrupt resolution for the Fenrir's alliance with his Father, Loki. They bound him, hoping to lure the Trickster out. They wanted him tried, brought to justice, and eventually brought to death. They hoped he would go to his son.

Now that they had the last Vitki in their possession, The Giant Fenrir, and Surt to their knees, they have turned the tides in their favor.

This was never foretold my Mimir, never written down by any skald, and never sung in any ballad. This was with the help of a Vitki and his Memory; of things that were never meant to be, but to be.

The end, not so

"Fjorn, it is time," said the soft voice whispering into his bleeding ears, "It is time to change the course, it is time for a new song," the voice was quiet, but Fjorn steadily listened, feeling the rope choke him harder, twisting around his throat. He felt the blood rush back to his head, he let out a gasp, breathing quickly, rapidly to the misty forest's pungent air.

He looked around for the voice, he could have sworn it was his wife's, his son's, people he loved who were no longer. He felt the rope tighten every time he opened his eyes, fluttering to the dense fog that blinded him more. He could see the world around him.

"It is time," said the voice again, two voices now together in a melody that brought joy to his ears.

He wiped the blood off of his ears, still dangling from the tight rope around his red neck. He opened his eyes to nothing, seeing nothing, he was blind, but he sensed there was more in the forest than sight would have given him.

He ripped the rope off the old branch, dropping down to the mud below. Rabbits, birds, squirrels fluttering away to the sound. He felt the earth below him, he felt the mud on his fingertips, the blood that dripped from every open wound, and he felt something more… something he could not explain to anyone else − He felt his wife's presence, "Is that you?" He asked through a broken throat, "I feel you once more," he choked, rubbing his burning throat. The skin was mangled, bone showing.

Nothing but the silent winds of the forest streamed graciously through the old woods. He felt the dying woods, the crying children far away, and the birth of life. He felt his wife's cool hands touching his back. He cried to himself, "I missed you," he wiped the tears out of his sightless eyes, "Oh, how I missed you."

"Your story is not over, Fjorn," the voice sounding more and more like his dead wife's. It brought more tears to him, but he remembered the word's Odin spoke to him and still spoke to him, words repeating over and over and over, *keep your wits at bay, Fjorn. For if you don't, the enemy will strike.*

He picked himself up from the muddy soil, rubbing his branded eyes, burning, aflame with the blue embers he bore before.

He remembered Ahlifer's long amber hair, the way it fluttered to the morning sun, the crisps of it when the sun stayed onto it too long.

Inga also, how stubborn, how cold, how much she was like her Mother−her nose. He remembered all of his loved ones not like the distant memories they were, but now companions closer to him.

Keep your wits at bay, Fjorn. For if you don't, the enemy will strike.

The voice again.
Now, it was truly the All-Father.

His Song had just begun,
His story had just been opened,
His memories,
Now truly alive.

Thank you.

Sincerely,
Bryce Carlson

Copyrighted.

Made in the USA
Monee, IL
24 March 2020